Minuet

THROUGH

Time

Adriana Dardan

authorHOUSE®

AuthorHouse™
1663 Liberty Drive
Bloomington, IN 47403
www.authorhouse.com
Phone: 1 (800) 839-8640

Published by AuthorHouse 04/09/2018

ISBN: 978-1-5462-3694-8 (sc)
ISBN: 978-1-5462-3693-1 (e)

Contents

Dedicated to the brave women who made a daring stride forward, and fought for their lives and the lives of their children in a world where the rule of man is forceful and decisive.

Adriana Dardan

FOREWORD

It is said that writing is an art that only few amateurs have the skill to honor it. Writers come in a wide range of talents, from none all the way up, to the highest elevation of a worldwide-recognized merit of excellence. The audience comes also in a wide range of readers who some are concerned with a gripping plot, while others search for a more subtle, less frenziedly-placed plot which evolves more farther down the surface.

Some very highly educated writers use a sophisticated style with noisy sounds and less meaning of the words. The readers in this category will benefit mostly from a lesson in linguistic rather than from a good writing. Some other writers use only the realistic side of a plot that revolve around the daily realities of life as experienced by regular people who can be encountered anytime in any place. The readers are stuck to a gloomy plot evolving around obscure characters who are not concerned with what they think and what they feel. Finally, some other writers combine a simple style with a plot part real and part imagined; the characters revolve around the daily experiences of life, focusing in the same time on an imaginary site where new meanings to express their thoughts and feelings become essential. These are the writers whose works are the most valued by readers.

Although this novel is a fictional endeavor, the succession of incidents was inspired by many real stories that occur in every spot of the world with similar developments. This story honors the life and struggle of a victim of domestic abuse who becomes a fugitive, running for her life and for the life of her child. The characters in the narrative evolve with the storyline where every day becomes a new page of a distinctive event. From the bottom of harshness, humiliation, derision, and fright, new hopes and new visions for a better future arise. The courage and sacrifices revealed by the main character are in the final part of the story, rewarded and revenged.

It is up to the Reader to assign the right classification of this narrative in one of the three groups mentioned above, or in to none of them after consideration.

Adriana Dardan

CHAPTER 1

Daring Steps

The little boy was only five years old when he pressed the button for emergencies call. His mother was lying on the kitchen floor in a pool of blood, without moving at all, as if she was dead. He tried to answer very clearly to all the questions the woman on the line asked him, keeping as much as he could the calm he needed without breaking into a devastating crisis.

"What is your name?"

"Justin."

"Do you know, Justin, who did this to your mother?"

"My father."

"Where is he now?"

"He left."

"Were you in the house?"

"No. I ran outside to our neighbor, Mrs. Morris, and then when I saw my father leaving I ran back to the house. I'm scared."

"Don't be. The ambulance is at your door. Go open it. Would you like me to stay on the line?"

"No need. Thank you. Door is open. Mrs. Morris just came to be with me and my mom."

He went to the door and let in the two men carrying their medical kit who asked him where the injured person was. He showed them the way to the kitchen where his mother was still not moving:

"Is she going to be all right?", he asked.

"She will, but we have to take her to the hospital quickly", one of the men answered.

They revived her, making sure that she could breathe and say a few words. It was not for the first time when they came to that house and rushed that poor woman to the hospital, but this time it seemed that she was very badly beaten up.

"I'm coming with you", the little boy said.

"Very well, come", one of the paramedics answered.

"We'll follow you with my car", Mrs. Morris said, "I cannot leave him alone."

She was in her late forties, short, chubby, and quick moving; a widow living alone, she had a nice house with a small garden, and her only family was a cat. Quite a few times already, she took care of the child who ran to her house asking protection against his father.

The hospital was only two blocks away and it took only a few minutes for the ambulance to get there. The injured woman was rushed to the emergency room, was surrounded by doctors and nurses, and was given all the care she needed. Only after a couple of hours, the doctor came out and approached the woman keeping the little boy asleep in her arms. He woke up when the doctor said:

"She will be all right, but she was severely injured. Her face will bear deep scars that will never disappear, her nose was broken and needs surgery, one of her eyes will remain smaller than the other, she has a cracked rib, and lots of bruises on her body. Overall, for now she needs all the care to heal her wounds, but later on she will need plastic surgery to restore her traits."

He addressed the little boy:

"Your mother will be all right this time. What is your name?"

"Justin Benson. She is everything I have. If she dies, I'll die too."

"She is not going to die, Justin, but you have to take care of her."

"I will, and I promise. Thank you, Sir."

The doctor approached Mrs. Morris, took her on the side, and whispered.

"There will be no next time. She lost a lot of blood and barely escaped alive. It is urgent that she takes her son and both run away, far from that monster, or they both will die by his hands. We contacted the authorities, they arrested him for a couple of days, but they cannot do anything unless she presses charges; I know from many similar cases that she never will. Now she is heavily sedated and we'll keep her overnight. Tomorrow I'll check her bandages and maybe you will take her home in the afternoon. Bye now and take care of yourselves."

Mrs. Morris and Justin returned home when it was already night. She kept him in her house, put him to bed, and prayed to Heavens for his protection.

The next morning Justin went to his kindergarten program, and Mrs. Morris tried to concentrate on her daily tasks without succeeding very well. She was terribly worried about her dear friend and the little boy, not knowing at all where to ask for help or at least an advice. In the afternoon, she told Justin that they have to go to the hospital and take home his mom.

"She has lots of bandages on her face, and I want you not to be scared when you'll see her. Can you behave like a big boy?"

"Yes. I just want her home, being safe and live in peace. I'm not scared looking at her bandages. I'm scared of my father when he will come home drunk again, screaming, and beating up my mom, as he did so many times. What are we going to do, Mrs. Morris?"

"We have to keep up our hopes that one solution must exist to solve this very complicated situation. We have to seek for help and we'll not give up until we'll find one. Let's go now."

They arrived at the hospital after only few minutes and went directly to the room. His mother opened her arms and Justin rushed over to her. She had tears in her eyes but he couldn't see them, while Mrs. Morris was to the point of crying.

"How are you, Andrea?", she asked. "We were terribly worried. Everything at home is all right for now. Are you ready to go? I wish you both stay with me for a little while. What do you think?"

"Thank you Matilda for everything, especially for taking care of Justin. I think that it would be better for us to stay in our home, because I know what will follow now. Marc will apologize, begging forgiveness, and making promises like always before. For the time being, we'll be safe. In the meantime, I'll think to find a solution to these terrible situations that keep repeating over and over again. Believe me, this time I'm decided to end this misery definitely."

The doctor showed up.

"Take your medication as I prescribed, to prevent any complication. Do not touch the bandages. Come after one week from now, to check your condition and see what we are doing next. Take good care of yourself."

He left with many doubts in his mind.

They went home and Mrs. Morris prepared dinner for them, making sure that both have enough to eat even if no one showed any appetite.

"May I sleep next to you?", Justin asked his mother.

"Yes, my dearest, I'll even try to tell you a bedtime story like every night before. If I fall asleep then you'll continue the story. Let's both thank to Mrs. Morris for her care and kindness. She must be very tired for so much tension we all have been through."

They both embraced the gentle woman and went to bed hoping for the next day to be better than the last ones.

Andrea started to tell her son the story of *the hare*

and the turtle, but she fell asleep long before ending it. Justin was still awake and he was thinking how fortunate were some of his classmates who had a father caring for them, playing ball with them, taking them to the park, and hugging them all the time. He also thought about those kids who don't have a father at all, and were more fortunate than he was who had a very bad one. Somehow, that very young boy made a stride in his life, and entered the world of the grown ups much too early. Before falling asleep, he added a few words to his nighttime prayer. His mother taught him that his prayer is a very private conversation between him and his Creator, and not even his mother should know about it. Even so, he will ask her first thing in the morning about the words he added to his prayer. With these thoughts in his mind, he fell asleep.

They both felt a little better in the morning after a good night rest. Andrea called the Dean's office at the university where she was a professor of French Culture and English Literature. She told the secretary, without giving any details, that she had an accident, and was unable to work for a while. At least, for the time being she found a cover for her absence. Justin was ready to go to his kindergarten class, but before, he said to his mother:

"Last night I added a few words to my prayer and I made it a little longer. You taught me not ever to pray for bad things to happen, but only for what is good and can be blessed. I prayed to my God Creator to protect my father from me, because I intend to kill him if he will strike you again. I think this is good and can be blessed. What do you think, Mom?"

"Oh, dear. This is not good at all and cannot be blessed. In your prayer you asked protection for your father against you, but how will be you protected if you become a killer? You will be miserable for the rest of your life, carrying in your soul the burden of a sin, which never can be erased. I commend you for being so honest and telling the truth in your prayer but, take off the words you added and keep your prayer the way you said it until now. People do very bad things and sooner or later punishment comes into their lives without us praying for a just retribution to be applied to them because of the evil they did. I know you are very worried about what is happening in our life. So am I. Nevertheless, I promise you to find a solution to end this situation and make a good and peaceful living for us both. Do you understand what I'm saying?"

"I think I do."

She caressed his beautiful face, thinking that not even a grown up would have found such a subterfuge to fill his need for revenge against the monster who became his father. Because of the precarious conditions in which he was compelled to live, somehow a tiny circuit in his brain became mature at his very young age, much ahead the right time.

By the end of the day, Marc showed up. He had a terrified expression on his face when he saw his wife. Kneeling before her, he tried to put some words together:

"I am terribly sorry for what I did to you. Please

forgive me. I swear not ever to do it again. I beg you to forgive me, my dearest Andrea. Can you?"

"Certainly, I forgive you. Let's have dinner, and talk something else."

She needed a detailed plan to escape that brute, and she had to be extremely careful for each move to follow out. Her attitude will be quite friendly, avoiding any animosity, and hiding deep her intention to get out of that unbearable marriage as fast as possible. After a few days, she had to go to the hospital to remove the bandages of her face. Before that, she had to prepare Justin for any unpleasant surprise and make sure that he will not be scared of her mutilated face. In that evening, Andrea asked him to sit next to her and have a little talk.

"Tomorrow I have to go to the hospital to get the bandages off my face. I would very much like you to come with me, because I'll be more comfortable knowing that I have you close to me. Would you come with me?"

"Of course I would. I'll be next to you all the time and I'll hold your hand, so that you'll not be scared."

"You're a very brave little boy, and I'm very proud of you. Thank you for understanding me so well."

In the next morning, they went to the hospital and Andrea explained to the doctor the reason for which she brought her son along.

"Very good thinking, Andrea. Let's do it together and very slowly."

He caressed the boy's head and said:

"Justin, I'm very glad to see you, and both, you

and I, we'll take the bandages off your mother's face, but before, the good nurse here will help you wash thoroughly your little hands. Agree?"

"Yes, Sir Doctor."

He asked Andrea to sit on a specially designed chair, and the nurse brought a high stool for Justin, next to the doctor. On the side, a mirror was set for Andrea, to follow all the moves the doctor will make.

"Let's start", he said.

With a special scissor he cut first a small part of the bandage until a little of a narrow scar showed up.

"Justin, put your fingers here, with a very gentle touch, and tell me how it feels."

"A little rough, but it's not frightening as I thought."

"Very good. Let's go a bit farther."

He cut another piece of the bandage and told Andrea to look in the mirror. She didn't say a word. Her breathing went faster and her mind was in a state of great commotion. The doctor cut little pieces of the bandage, and asked Justin again to touch the scars.

He started trembling and saw his mother having tears in her eyes. Nevertheless, he was there to be close to her and making sure, that she will not be scared. With lot of shyness, he touched all the scars the doctor showed him, and with big effort, he managed to master the emotion that overwhelmed him.

"You will be all right, Mom. Your face is a little different than it was, but this doesn't change at all my love for you. Later, you'll have surgery to make you beautiful as you were before. Don't worry; I'll take care of you."

Now, everybody in the room was ready to cry. Could a grown up person make a more sensitive statement? Hard to believe.

All the bandages were taken off Andrea's face when she took a long look in the mirror without saying a word, without crying, without showing a sign of anger. She just had to accept her fate as it was.

Taking her son in her arms, she embraced him with all the love of her heart.

"Let's go home, my dearest."

The doctor gave her some instructions to follow and they were about to leave when the nurse approached her and whispered:

"Call this number from a public phone. When you hear a voice on the line, say only the word '*petunia*'. You will get instructions to follow. This is an underground organization helping women and children who have been heavily abused. You and your child will be safe."

She turned around and left without saying another word. They went home and Andrea already had a plan to follow. She only had to work carefully on the details. Marc was not home yet, and she didn't expect anything else but a situation of mutual hostility, for which she was well prepared. Suddenly, her gaze turned to the photograph on the desk. She and Marc looked at each other, smiling. Andrea had a feeling of nostalgia when she thought about the good times they both cherished and valued. She was about twenty-three years old and he was twenty-seven when they got married. She just was offered the position of Assistant Professor of French Culture and English Literature at the university, and he worked as Senior Editor with a reputable Publishing Company. They fell in love at first sight when they met at a symposium for the discussion of the academic English language. She was of an unusual beauty, with blond, wavy hair, dark blue eyes, very fine traits, and when she smiled, people said that the sun became brighter. Marc was no less good looking, especially when he talked about a subject that he mastered with considerable ability and his eyes and face radiated cheerfulness to a great degree. His mother was the only family he had, but she lived alone somewhere on the East coast. Her parents died in an automobile accident two years before, and she had no family left. Shortly after getting married, they bought a comfortable house in the city of Santa Barbara, hoping together to built a family and having a long, happy life. When Justin was born, they both had the greatest joy of their life together. All that state of joy and happiness lasted only about four years. One day Marc applied for the position of Chief Editor, but someone else took the job. He got angry and beat the director of the company so hard that he put him in the hospital. Marc ended up in jail for a while, and he came out a different man. He started drinking, became abusive, and nothing from his good nature was left. He was in and out of jobs because of his drinking problem and his aggressive attitude. With every passing day, their life together became worse, without any perspective for improvement. Andrea tried hard all the time to change the entire situation for the better, but she had not a bit of success. She asked him for a divorce, but he said that he rather would kill her before he will agree to divorce her. Their beautiful love was slowly fading away, leaving no trace behind. She remembered that almost every evening Marc asked her to play piano for him. He liked especially *Chopin* and she was a very good piano player. Many times, since Justin was only about three years old, she took him on her lap and taught him to play the notes and short pieces composed for small children. A little later, he learned how to read musical notes, much before he learned the alphabet and how to read and write. By the same time, she also gave him French lessons, and after only one year, he could communicate with his mother, using simple sentences. Justin was a very beautiful boy with emerald green eyes, slightly curled light brown hair, fair complexion, and a smile that could conquer the world. He inherited his mother's not only physical features, but also her nature. Marc loved to watch them both and kissed them with tenderness after the piano lesson was finished. It was long ago, and it was a happy time for the three of them.

After enduring many abuses and humiliation, and especially after the recent time when he disfigured her, she decided to give up on him, take her son, and disappear from his life forever.

Late in that evening, Marc came home, drunk, and ready to cast all his troubles upon her, as usually. When he saw her face, he started slurring and laughing, like having a big pleasure.

"Wow! You look so ugly and disgusting! Go away and don't show me your face again!"

Andrea didn't move and didn't utter a word. He went straight to bed and she went to the study to think about the details of the plan she was going to accomplish. She already knew exactly what she had to do.

Next morning, Marc left, probably looking for another job, while Andrea went to Mrs. Morris house after taking Justin to the kindergarten.

"I would like to have with you a few words, Matilda. You have been for a long time, a good friend, like family to Justin and me, but it came the right time for us to go away and start a new life. I cannot tell you any details because I don't know myself what I'll do next. The main thing is, that if you'll not see us anymore around the house, it means that we are gone. The less you know, the better will be for us all. Thank you, my friend for everything you done for us."

"I understand very well, Andrea, my dear friend. I admire your courage and only can say, be safe you and Justin, and may your soul be at peace."

They embraced each other, without making any promises for the future.

From there, Andrea went straight to the bank, took all the money she had in her personal savings deposit and closed the account. Her next step was to the university, and she went directly to the Dean's office. When he saw her, he had a small trembling.

"What happened to you, Andrea? What miserable beast did this to you?"

"I had an accident and please don't ask me to tell you the details, Professor Duncan. I came to give my resignation and this is extremely hard for me. As you can see, I will not be able to lecture in front of my students with this face, talking about the beauty of French art and of the English language. It takes time for me to heal and after that, I'll decide for a plastic surgery. I only hope that you will understand and accept my decision to give up for now the career I love and served with dignity and honesty."

"I honor your decision, my dear, but you don't know how sorry I am. If ever you'll be ready to come back, your position will be always here for you. Goodbye, Andrea. Take care of you and may you find the right path to go in your life."

She left with sadness, knowing well that there was no way for her to come back. It was time for Justin to come from his kindergarten. Andrea went there and talked to his teacher, saying that for the time being Justin will live with his grandmother out of state and will be unable to attend the program. They went home just in time for them both to have a very important talk:

"What I am about to tell you is strictly confidential and no one has to find out. I took the decision for us to leave and go away. I'm expecting you to behave properly, to understand that there is no other solution for us to be safe, and also, to trust me entirely with everything I have to decide for our future. Tomorrow,

I'll find where we'll be going and I'll let you know every single detail about what we are supposed to do. Did you understand what I told you?"

"Perfectly. I am a big boy now, and not a baby. Whatever you decide I know that will be the best for us both."

He ran into his mother's arms, like sealing for good a promise that will never be broken.

Late evening, Marc came home and went straight to bed, without saying a word this time. Andrea made sure that he was asleep without any chance to wake up soon. She went outside to the first public phone and made the call. A woman voice answered after a few rings.

"*Petunia*", Andrea said, and waited. The voice asked for her address and Andrea gave it to her. Then the voice said:

"Take all your personal papers, pack one single quite small suitcase with clothes, and do not take any photos or souvenirs. Tomorrow at ten o'clock evening, get into the black car at the corner of the street, without asking questions and without talking to the driver."

The phone was silent and Andrea understood that she got all the instructions she had to follow. She just made the first daring steps toward an unknown future.

Back home, she tried without any success to get some sleep, thinking that tomorrow will be a hard and long day for her and Justin.

Early in the morning, they all had breakfast and Marc seemed to be in a better mood because he said that he will go for an interview hoping to get a good job. He left in a hurry around nine o'clock leaving Andrea and Justin to take care of what was very important to them.

"Let's pack our stuff carefully because we cannot take too much", Andrea said.

In a medium-size suitcase, she put some clothes for her and Justin, all the personal papers they needed and one book for Justin that he liked most. It was the month of January, outside was still a pleasant weather, but she didn't know where they will be going, and therefore she took also some warm clothes in case they will have to live in a cold region. The money she had was supposed to last for a few months covering housing and food, in case she will not be able to find a job. She was not supposed to take any photos, but still she found a small one showing her with Justin in her arms when he was two years old; she took that picture, hiding it with the money in the travel belt around her waist. Everything was ready. Andrea said:

"Late tonight, we are going to sneak out on the street and get into the car that will be waiting for us. We are not supposed to say a single word, or ask the driver where we are going. We will keep silence along that trip all the way, until we'll arrive to our destination. There, we'll receive new instructions to follow. It is very important to remember this: there also, we'll receive new papers with different names such that no one could find us. This might sound like a lie to you and I always taught you to tell only the truth. Nevertheless, there are situations when you are allowed to tell a lie, and this is only, and I repeat, only when your life or the life of someone dear to you is in danger. It is the case now, when we'll have to change our identities and leave behind the truth about our names, home, school, and friends. Everything I told you before, and just now, have to be carried out, according to the minute details of our plan. Agree?"

"Completely. I understood every single word you said and I know exactly what I'm supposed to do."

"Very good. Let's have a final look and check everything and everywhere, to see if we missed something."

Many things they would have liked to take with them, but they couldn't. They looked around with sadness, knowing very well that it was for the last time, and they will not see again the place called "home" where they had many happy moments to remember and treasure.

It was already evening when Marc came back. He was in a very bad mood, drunk, and refused to join them for dinner. He couldn't get the job, went to a bar, and threw his anger in to many drinks. After some cursing words he spit on those two, and barely standing on his feet, he went to bed.

Andrea knew very well that he will fall into a deep sleep without moving until morning. It was almost ten o'clock when she took Justin by one hand and the suitcase with the other, and both sneaked outside. They walked to the corner of the street where the black car was waiting for them. Without a word, the driver showed them inside, and started the car. After a while,

Justin fell asleep in his mother's arms. Andrea had no idea where that road was going, nor was she aware of the places they were traveling through. After more than one hour, the car stopped in front of a small building. The driver said:

"Go to the door and knock five times."

Andrea woke up her son, took the suitcase, went to the door, and knocked five times. A woman in her fifties probably, opened, and showed them inside a small room. She had an uneven step and walked with a limp.

"Have a seat. Give me all your papers", the woman said, and she called someone on the phone.

A short man with white hair came in. They both looked at the papers, whispered to each other, then the man took pictures of both Andrea and Justin, and left taking the papers with him.

"It would be better for the boy to get some sleep on that couch, since is very late, he is tired, and he is not in the shape to be questioned.

Andrea took Justin in her arms and did what the woman said, covering the boy with a blanket, after which she took a seat in front of a small desk.

"Your new papers will be ready in the morning. You and the boy will have new identities and you both will forget the names you have now and the place you came from. You will be sent to an undisclosed location where housing and food are paid for two weeks, after which you are on your own. You can stay in that area, or you can go farther on, and this will be your choice.

You will never use the phone and you will not contact anybody from your family or friends. You will never mention anything to anyone about this organization. You will make the best you can to find a job to support the two of you, trying to save the money you have now. Wherever you and your son will choose to live, keep a low profile as much as you can. Don't trust anybody, no matter how good or friendly someone might be. One time or the other that person could utter a misplaced word and you can end up dead. Your husband will do everything in his power to search for you two, reporting to the police your disappearance, and abduction of his son. Watch where you go, to whom you talk, and avoid any crowded places, especially those with television sets, because you can be sure that yours and your son's pictures will be publicized as 'missing persons wanted by the police'. If you suspect something wrong, take your son and move to another place, city, or town. The best for you would be a big city, where you can be less noticed, find an inexpensive place to stay, a job, and a school for your son. These instructions cover about all I had to tell you. If you are careful as I said, you and your son will be safe. This is your only chance to survive, and there is no other one. Tomorrow morning I'll question your son, and give him the instructions he has to follow. After that, you will be ready to go to your new location, and you'll find out there what is next for you to do. Now, try to get some sleep in that armchair, for the rest of the night."

The woman left without saying any other word, and

Andrea sat in the armchair as she was told. Her mind was swirling of so many blurred thoughts coming back and forth with nothing clear and steady. She was very tired and fell asleep, but only for few minutes. It was early in the morning when another woman entered the room and showed Andrea the chair in front of the desk, asking her to sit down.

"Wake up your boy and ask him to join us."

Andrea did was she was told, woke up her son and brought him to a chair next to her. He was still sleepy but didn't say anything.

"Here are your new papers with new identities for you and your son", the woman said. "From this moment on, your name is 'Lara Collins'. The birthday and birthplace are written in your papers, you have to memorize them and completely forget the old ones."

She addressed Justin:

"Your mother explained to you why you are here, what do you have to do, and what will be your responsibilities from now on. Your name from this moment on is 'Adam Collins'. You have to exercise, saying it repeatedly, until you'll feel comfortable and be sure that you will not use the name you had before. Your new birthday is written on this paper, you are now one year older, and your birthday place is Philadelphia. You have to memorize also this information until you feel comfortable. One time or another, someone might ask you about your father. You will tell that you don't know your father because he died little after you were born. This is of course a lie, but you have to accept it even if you don't feel comfortable. Did you understand everything I just told you? If you have questions, feel free to ask without hesitation."

"I understood very well, Madame, everything you said, and I promise to take responsibility for memorizing all you told me, and not making any mistakes."

"I have to ask you if you know the difference between truth and lie. Do you?"

"Yes, I know. I always have to tell the truth but sometimes I am allowed to tell a lie, and this is only, when my life or the life of someone dear to me is in danger. It is the case now, when we'll have to change our identities and leave behind the truth about our names, home, school, and friends. This is what my mother taught me." He just repeated what Lara explained to him.

"You are a very bright boy, Adam. You understood very well everything I said. You and your mother will be safe from now on and you both will have a better life."

A young girl showed up, bringing two boxes with food.

"Lara", the woman continued talking, "here is your breakfast before you're leaving. After that, the driver will take you to the interstate bus station. Your destination will be a small town called 'Parker' on the Arizona border. Someone will be waiting for you there, and you will have new instructions to follow. To be recognized, that person will say the word 'gladiola' and you will answer with the word 'dandelion'. Do you have any questions?"

"No. We both thank you for everything you did for us."

"Go in peace", the woman said and she left.

After having their breakfast and freshened up, they went outside where the same driver was waiting in the car. He drove them to the bus station, bought the tickets, and helped them to get into the bus.

"It will take about four hours for the bus to get there. You can have a nice rest. Good luck", he said, and left without any other word.

Lara and Adam took their seats in the bus and after about half hour their journey to a new location started. It was the first time since last night when they could talk alone.

"Are you all right?", Lara whispered.

"Yes, Mom, at least I think so. You know, I'm still a little scared about what will happen to us."

"I feel the same, but I cannot tell you anything because I don't know more than that lady told us. We'll find out when we'll arrive to our new destination and from there we'll go step by step, making sure that we do the right thing."

"You're right. Until then we just have to wait."

"You know what? Let's get some sleep. I didn't have much last night."

"I'll try, since anyway, there is nothing exciting or interesting to look outside. I remember that I didn't have the chance to say goodbye to Mrs. Morris, and I regret."

"I said it for you. Now let's get some sleep."

After about three hours they woke up, more refreshed and with a better frame of mind. They both were hungry but had nothing to eat. Looking outside, Adam exclaimed:

"Look there! Those people seem to have a big party with music and dance! Certainly, they don't have troubles like us."

"They have probably, but decided to forget about what was unpleasant in their lives and chose to have a good time for a while. Every one has trouble, one way, or the other, my dear."

Shortly after, the bus stopped at the final destination, the town called "Parker", and all the passengers were asked to step out. A short man in his late sixties approached the two refugees, and said:

"Gladiola."

"Dandelion", Lara answered.

"Welcome to our beautiful little town. You can call me Nick."

"Thank you for your kind greeting, Nick. I am Lara, and this is my son Adam".

"I am very pleased to meet you both. Let's go to my house and make you feel comfortable in your new location."

They stepped into the car and only after ten minutes of drive, they arrived to a nice, small house surrounded by lots of flowers and trees. A woman about the same age showed up and greeted them.

"Welcome to our home. You must be tired and

hungry since is already past lunchtime. Let's go inside. Call me Beth."

"Thank you Beth for your kindness", Lara said, and stated hers and Adam's names.

The house was small but very neat and well maintained.

"You will be staying in the dwelling behind our house, which you can see from here. Your temporary residence and food are paid for two weeks. After that, you'll make a decision how to go further on. Let's eat first, and then we'll show you the place."

She put on the table some cooked dishes, salads, and fruits. The two newcomers showed a big appetite, not paying any attention to the couple who stared at them with empathy. After lunch, the couple escorted them to the place where they were supposed to start a new life. The small house had one tiny bedroom with two miniature beds, a bathroom, and a kitchenette only big enough to accommodate one person. The place was clean and comfortable.

"It is more than we expected" Lara said. "For the time being we only need to get familiarized with our new mode of living. Thank you both for everything."

"You are welcome", Beth said. "Dinner is served at seven o'clock. Until then you can unpack your stuff, get some rest, or feel free to walk in the yard. I suggest not trying the streets, yet. If you need anything, please feel free to ask. We both are here to help you. We'll see you later."

They left. Lara and Adam started looking around, not knowing exactly what to do first.

"Let's start unpacking and then go outside for some fresh air", Lara said.

They put only some of their belongings in closet, leaving most of them in the suitcase. Outside was a mild, dry winter time, and the Colorado river could be spotted not far from their place. The yard was quite large, enough for them to walk back and forth several times. There were no people on the street and everything was quiet and very pleasant.

"What will be next for us to do?", Adam asked.

"We'll stay about two weeks here, we'll go visiting the town, and if we like it, I'll look for a job and we can stay longer. I cannot teach anymore and I cannot hope to find a good job with my face, no matter how low paid. However, maybe there is something, somewhere for me too. For the time being, we have enough money to live for a while. Still, I'm thinking that this little, nice town is too close to what was our home, and I feel like it would be safer for us to go farther, to a bigger city with more chances for me to find a job."

"You're right as always. We'll see how these two weeks will be for us."

"Yes, my dearest, we'll wait and see. You know what came out good from all this mess in which we got involved? According to your new birth certificate, you are now one year older, meaning that you can start going to school, this coming fall."

Adam's face radiated with joy. He started jumping up and down like a little savage.

"This makes me very happy. I started getting bored of so much kindergarten. I can't wait to go to a real school and be able to learn many interesting things."

"I'm happy too. We have to find a steady place to live until then in a big city, a job for me, and a good school for you. Knowing to read and write already, it could make the first grade to be not so interesting for you; did you think about this side?"

"Anything will be more interesting than kindergarten. Besides, there must be some subjects for me to learn and appreciate without getting bored."

"I think so too. We have about seven months till then, in which time we'll acquire a lot of knowledge about our new lifestyle. Now, let's go inside, take a shower, and watch television until dinner."

On the nightstand, Lara found a tourist guide with maps and indications for the main attractions in town. She intended to use it next day.

A little before seven o'clock they went to dinner, being received with kindness and a big smile by their hosts. A casual conversation over a frugal meal, made a pleasant atmosphere appreciated by everybody.

"Is everything all right with your accommodations?", Beth asked. "If you need anything just say it without hesitation".

"Everything is fine and above expectations. I'll appreciate if you have a local newspaper, and let me take a look, maybe I can find a job. With my face, I don't raise my hopes, but anyway, I want to try."

"Here is one", Nick said, "you can take it and have a look at the adds. This is a very small town and jobs are scarce, but there is no harm to look for one."

Lara and Adam went back to their place after Beth told them that breakfast will be served between seven and nine o'clock. The newspaper was mostly filled with ads for tourism showing some places where people can enjoy and relax. There were only two requests for jobs and those were for strong men to do heavy lifting in a warehouse building.

Mother and son had a good night sleep, feeling much better and safer than before. In the morning after breakfast, they went for a walk following the indications in the tourist guide, and arrived to "La Paz County Park" on the Colorado River. Sites showed some diversities and perhaps the best ones mentioned in the guide were the dry camping sites next to the river. Most sites either were on the water or had water views. Across the street, they could see a golf course where only a few people were playing. A small place with tables outside tempted them to have lunch instead of going back to the house. There was not much to see, and they returned to the house in time for dinner after taking a long walk along the river.

Next morning they went to visit the Indian Tribes Museum where they could learn a little bit about the tribes that lived near the Colorado River for thousands of years. The museum was small but had a beautiful collection of artifacts, including crafts and pottery made by Aboriginals.

"I think that it will be better for us to leave and find a bigger town to stay", Lara said. "There is nothing here for us, I cannot find a job, and we are only wasting a precious time. What do you think?"

"You're right. Let's go somewhere else and maybe everything will be better for us."

"We'll pack our stuff and tomorrow morning we'll head toward Phoenix."

In that evening, Lara talked to Nick and Beth, telling her decision to leave.

"Would it be much trouble for you to give us a ride to the bus station?", she asked Nick.

"No trouble at all, but why don't you stay a little longer? You still have housing and food paid for ten more days."

"Thank you both for your kindness, but we should not forget that we are not here on vacation, and is urgent for me to find a job and a place to stay. I decided to head toward Phoenix."

"We understand, and perhaps you took the right decision. Tomorrow morning I'll drive you to the bus station, after we'll see the departure time to Phoenix."

The next morning they were ready to leave, when Beth showed up with a big bag with food:

"You'll have here enough for the entire day and maybe for tomorrow too. I regret that you only stayed with us for such a short time, but you took a right decision and I'm sure everything will be all right for you both. Goodbye now and go in peace."

They embraced each others and the two fugitives arrived at the station right in time to get the bus.

The trip to Phoenix lasted about two and a half hours. Very few people were around when they arrived. They spotted a motel nearby that seemed to be a good place to start their sojourn. It was a small, neat building, and a friendly woman at the desk welcomed with kindness their arrival. She noticed Lara's face but seemed not to give it any attention. Her only reaction was a small trembling. She gave them a room at the second floor and answered to all the questions Lara asked, regarding streets guide, distance to downtown, and the nearest shopping center.

The room was nicely furnished with two small beds, a bathroom, and a view of the street.

"This is very comfortable", Adam said, "and that lady was very nice to us. Don't you think so?"

"Yes, I think so too. Let's unpack just the stuff we need now, and tomorrow we'll go looking for a place to rent. After that, we'll look for a daycare where you can stay, and I'll search for a job around. How this plan sounds to you?"

"Sounds good, except for the daycare. I can very well stay home alone while you are working, and you don't have to worry about me at all. I don't like the idea of playing with small children and learning how to draw balloons and flowers, sitting on the floor."

"We'll find a daycare where children about your age

are admitted. You cannot stay alone all day long until I come home from work. Besides, I'll not be able to do my job properly, while being worried about you all the time. Think about this also, please."

He mumbled something, without saying loud what he thought. When she took a decision, he knew well that he had no chance for arguing.

In the afternoon, they went outside for a walk just to become familiar with the neighborhood. At a magazine stand, Lara bought a street guide map of the city, a local newspaper, and a couple of children publications for Adam.

"The plan we made", she said, "has to be divided in sections according to priorities. First thing is to find a daycare center, then around that area we'll look for an apartment, and after that I'll search for a job close to both places. Agree?"

"Yes, and I hope we'll find everything the way you planned."

"I have to mention you something of great importance. I will not be able to find a teaching job, or a job in an office, or not even in a store, because the look of my face. I only can work in a place without people around to see me, and this will be probably a low paid job as a house cleaner in a motel or hotel. I hope you understand and you will not be disappointed. How do you feel about this perspective?"

"I understand and I'm not disappointed for me, because no matter how you look and what you do for a job, I love you the same. I am disappointed for you, because you liked so much teaching back home, you used to tell me always how pleased you were with your students, and you told me many stories about your work. Now, you have nothing of all that and this worries me a lot."

She took him in her arms and tried hard not to burst in to tears.

"I cannot make any promise in this regard because I don't know if I can keep it. However, I must tell you that my dearest wish is to be able in good time to have surgery, which will restore my face to its former features. In any event, my strongest wish of all is to do everything in my power for you to have the best education one can have, which will make you feel proud, contented, and self-confident. This is a promise I make to you and I know that I can keep it."

She was not shy at all to use words that would be hard to understand for other children at his age. Since he was born, she talked to him a lot, telling him stories, to encourage his curiosity for learning new words and new meanings of expressions.

As a reaction to what she said, his eyes gleamed with joy, and kissed her both cheeks with love.

"I promise to be always as you taught me, which is being good, honest, and considerate."

"This makes me very proud, and I can say that you and I, we both make a very good team. Now, let's have some sleep because tomorrow we have many things to do."

She looked at him while he was asleep, and thought

that indeed, she will do everything in her power to give him the highest education one can have. He will take over from a much higher level than the one from which she fell so low, and made her to accept the deplorable circumstances that she couldn't prevent. She had a sturdy education and a brilliant career, which both became of no further use for her. A low paid job, in a dirty place, that was all she could expect, maybe for the rest of her life. What was still allowed for her to do, was to concentrate her entire energy on the future of her son. He will have everything to achieve a high position in society, exceeding the common measure of his generation, above and beyond the greatest expectations of his own mother. She made a solemn promise and she will keep it. With these thoughts in her mind, she fell asleep, smiling.

In the morning, both woke up in a very good mood and ready to start the day as they planned.

"I'm hungry and there is not much food left in the bag that Beth gave us", Adam said.

"How about hot chocolate and pancake?"

"Sounds very good and I haven't such a delight in a long time. Where can we find something like that?"

"There is an eatery across the street; let's go there and see, but before, I would like to take all the information we need for everything we are going to do today."

In the phone book, Lara found the address of a daycare center located in downtown. She called and made an appointment. On the map of the city, she circled several street names with the intention to find an apartment and a job in that area. Ready to go out, they went to the eatery and had a hearty breakfast, after which they took the local bus to downtown from the corner of the street. In few minutes, they were in front of the daycare center. It was Friday, by the end of January.

"Watch what you say and be careful how you answer the questions", Lara said.

"I know, Mom. We exercised a lot and I remember everything. Don't worry."

A young woman answered to the door and let them in. She had a small trembling when saw Lara's face, but was very pleasant and liked Adam from the first time he started talking. Her name was Vanessa. She explained them everything about the facility and didn't ask any embarrassing questions. Only after few minutes, she liked Lara and felt much easier when looking directly at her face. The price was much lower than other daycare facilities and they had a wide variety of activities including art, computer lab, gym, and even field trips. They took the children to movies, swimming, and educational facilities and it didn't cost any extra. At the end of the interview, they agreed for Adam to start the program in the next coming week from eight to six.

"I think it's a nice place, like a school, and she is very pleasant", Adam said before his mother asked him what he thought.

"I'm very glad that you like it, and I'm sure that you will feel very good among other children of your age.

The best part is that they have so many activities as she described. I'm happy that we found this place. Now, let's go find an apartment. We walk."

Lara looked at the map where she circled the area close to the daycare, but there were no signs for rent.

"Look!", Adam shouted, "We missed this one!"

Indeed, they passed a few minutes before by that building but didn't notice the sign. It was a two stories building, about six minutes far from the daycare. More running than walking they went at the door and rang the bell. A short man in his late sixties, with a chubby face, showed them in, without paying any attention to Lara's face. He was the manager and had a one bedroom apartment at the second floor, all furnished, and with the usual amenities. He showed them the way, and they both liked the place. Lara signed the agreement without hesitation and paid the rent for one month. They will move in by the first of February, which was after two days.

Outside, they both started jumping up and down for so much good fortune that happened to them.

"Now, let's find a job", Adam said.

"I'm thinking to do it next week. It is already afternoon, we'll go have lunch somewhere around, and go back to the motel. Monday you'll go to the daycare and I'll take our belongings and go to the apartment. Then, I have plenty of time to look for a job. What do you say?"

"Works for me, but I thought that you were anxious to find a job."

"I am, but I want to have plenty of time and not rush into something that it will not be good enough for me."

They went to a small restaurant owned by a Chinese couple who greeted them with a big smile. The food was excellent and they asked for a few more portions to take out.

Back to the motel, they followed the evening schedule and not too late, they went to bed.

Monday morning, Lara took Adam to the daycare, returned to the motel, and started packing their belongings. She left the motel without any regrets and went to the apartment. It was small but very comfortable. Outside was a pleasant weather, and she thought that walking was better than taking the bus. First, she went to a bank close by, opened an account since she had an address already, and in a safe deposit box she put the cash carried in her travel belt around her waist, keeping only a small amount for current needs. From there, she started walking the streets, hoping for a "help wanted" sign to show up.

It was already afternoon when she returned home, without any positive result. On her way back, she stopped by the store and bought some kitchen stuff, tableware, and food for the entire week, intending to start cooking. Looking through the window, she tried to put some order in her thoughts that were all blurred and gloomy. She was all alone without home, without job, without family, in a wide world with a small child in her hand, who needed her care and her entire courage to help him grow up.

"What am I going to do?", she asked herself. "What will happen to us if I cannot find a job? The money we still have might last for several months, and then what? Besides, I'm scared to death that Marc could find us, send me to prison, and take Adam. For the authorities, abduction will weigh more than my disfigured face, and certainly, they will not have any sympathy for me. I live in constant fear, trying hard to hide it from Adam."

Heavy tears started flowing down her marred cheeks. She stood there, in front of the window without being able to take a decision or at least to think clearly. Just to make her mind a little bit free from cloudiness, she started cooking. It was time for her to take Adam from the daycare when she finished. He had to learn to come home alone and that was another concern for her.

Lara opened her arms when Adam rushed to meet her at the door.

"I missed you", he said, "but I had a great time. Did you find a job?"

"No, my dearest, I didn't. I missed you too, a lot. Let's go home and we'll talk."

The teacher approached Lara with a big smile:

"Adam is a very bright kid, being familiar with many subjects of learning. I'm very happy to have him here. He mingled with the other children in only minutes, and showed them that he likes a lot their company."

"Thank you very much for the appreciation and your kindness", Lara said. "He is a good boy. We'll see you tomorrow."

Hand in hand, they walked home.

"How was your day?", Lara asked. "Do you like the place?"

"I like it very much, the teacher is very nice, and the children are friendly, even if a little too noisy. I learned today how fish swim and do not need to breathe like other creatures do. It was interesting. Miss Vanessa said that tomorrow we'll go to the museum of Natural Science and look at fossils. Now you tell me about your attempt to find a job."

They arrived home in good time for dinner.

"I looked around everywhere in the close area, but there were no signs for hiring. Tomorrow I'll go a little farther and do the same search. I cooked fresh dinner. How would you like baked chicken with potatoes and salad?"

"Very much, but I'm really worried about our situation and especially about you."

"Let me take care of our situation and of myself. Everything will be fine, but it takes a little time. Tomorrow is another day and I'll try again. You have to trust me and share with me all your thoughts that bother you."

The next morning she took him to the daycare and returned home to look on the map for an enlarged area of searching. Back on the streets, she took the bus this time and looked around for "help wanted" signs. There was none. Her strength started diminishing until she felt weak and unable to make any further efforts. She just had not enough willingness to make another attempt to find a job. Back home, she lay on the bed, thinking in vain what she was going to do next. It was already past noon when she thought to try the phone book and ask places where there might be some hiring. Since she had no phone, Lara went downstairs to ask the manager for a phone book. She rang at the door and a tall woman with gray hair, answered.

"My husband told me about renting you the apartment upstairs, but we didn't have the chance to meet. I am Diana Crawford. You can call me Diana. What can I do for you?"

"My name is Lara Collins, and I'm very glad to meet you, Diana. I need a phone book that I could take it upstairs for an hour or so, if it's not too much trouble."

"No trouble at all. Here is the phone book and you can keep it for as long as you need."

The woman took a long look at her before she said:

"I have seen many faces like yours. Don't have to be embarrassed. I know you're looking for a job and you can't find one around."

"Thank you for being so understanding. Yes, I'm looking for a job, hoping to find one close to the apartment and to the daycare where my son goes, but I couldn't find one. This is the reason I asked you for the phone book, because I'll try to call some places and maybe one will answer to me."

"I'll tell you what we are going to do", Diana said. "My sister is the owner and manager of the motel on the second street far from here. She is looking for help but she will not hire anyone without references. I'll give you a note and you'll go there and talk to her. She will have the references to hire you. What do you say?"

"I am astounded by your kindness and generosity, Diana. You just saved my child's life and mine. I don't know how to thank you enough."

"I'll tell you how. Just take care of you and your child and be aware all the time that you both are still in danger. That is all I can tell you, and I'm happy if I can help."

She wrote something on a paper, and gave it to Lara in an envelope, showing her the directions to the address of the motel.

Without wasting a minute longer, Lara rushed to the place indicated by Diana. It was indeed, quite close to the apartment and to the daycare center. It was a single floor long building, with a parking lot in front. Lara entered the lobby where at the desk she saw a woman busy with some papers. She had a long figure with a sharp nose, her hair was gray, and she looked like being in her early sixties.

"Good afternoon", Lara said, "my name is Lara Collins. Mrs. Diana Crawford sent me to see you for an interview regarding a job."

"She just told me on the phone about you coming to see me. Have you worked before as a maid?", her voice was harsh and low.

"No, Madame."

"I'll hire you for a period of trial. If after one week, you show me that you can do the job, I'll give you the permanent position. You'll have to clean ten rooms, and you'll get paid with minimum wage. The working hours are from nine to five with half hour break for lunch. You can start tomorrow and make sure that you don't show your face too openly before the patrons. My name is Mrs. Lena Wilson. Any questions?"

"No, Mrs. Wilson. Thank you very much for giving me a chance to work. I'll not disappoint you. Goodbye, and I'll be here tomorrow before nine."

Lara left with slow steps, but once outside on the street, she almost jumped of so much joy and rushed to take home her son. She arrived early, Adam was still in class, but he saw her through the window and ran outside, directly into her arms".

"You got it!", he shouted.

"Yes, I did! Let's go home."

Adam said goodbye to his teacher and joined his mother. On the way home, she told him everything.

"I'm so happy for us both!", he said.

"I'm happy too, especially that is close to home and to your school. I'll take you there in the morning before I go to work and take you home in the evening, and so you don't have to walk alone. This gives me great peace of mind. Tell me now, how was your day."

"We went to the museum and saw there many worms and bugs embedded in to rocks. Miss Vanessa told us that those creatures lived very long ago, much before people were born, but they disappeared along the time. We also saw skeletons of big reptiles and one of a huge dinosaur who lived long ago and disappeared because a comet struck the earth. It really was a very interesting class and I learned today many new things."

"I'm so happy that everything worked out so well for both of us. Now let's go to the store and buy some food for the entire week."

Both carrying lots of bags arrived home when it was already evening. Lara started cooking a few dishes, and Adam offered to help saying that he liked better talking with his mother than watching television. Both finished when it was almost time to go to bed.

Next morning they woke up early and were ready to go. Lara took Adam to school and she walked to her place of job, arriving there before nine o'clock.

Mrs. Wilson was in the lobby talking to a woman dressed in a working uniform.

"This is Martha", she said, "and she will show you around, instructing you how to do your job."

"I'm pleased to meet you, Martha. My name is Lara and I'll appreciate very much your help in starting my job."

They shook hands and smiled at each other. Martha was African-American, very good looking, especially that her eyes showed a particular warmth and she was smiling when she talked. She had a very strong body built like an athlete.

"Come, Lara. Let's start the day on the right foot. First, let's get you a uniform."

They went to a supply room filled with all kind of cleaning stuff, blankets, comforters, pillows, and bed sheets. Martha checked several sizes of uniforms and found the right one to fit Lara's body. After that, she showed her a cart and all the stuff that had to be loaded and checked every single morning.

"Take the cart and let's go and see the rooms assigned to you for cleaning."

They entered one of the rooms, which was just vacated. It was a real mess, starting with the bed and finishing with the shower. Martha went to the minute details explaining her where to start and how to do the job.

"The other nine rooms assigned to you are about the same. Finish this one, and then go to the next, but first make sure that there are no customers inside, because you are not supposed to disturb them. I let you work now, and if you need anything, I'll be at the end of the building in the first room. I'll come see you at break time. Have a good day, Lara."

"Thank you Martha, and see you later."

Lara looked around and started working as Martha told her. Most of the time she was on her knees, scrubbing, and searching for stained spots, being careful not to miss even the smallest ones. Until break time she already cleaned three rooms and there were four more to go in that day. Martha showed up and told her to join her for lunch.

"You did good", she said, "very good job, Lara."

"I'm trying not to disappoint Mrs. Wilson. Besides, if I do a good work, I am pleased with myself."

She took the small sandwich brought from home,

and followed Martha to a very small room where a round table and a few chairs were the only furniture.

Martha opened her lunch box and looked at Lara's meal.

"You are not going to last for long with only a tiny sandwich. If you intend to work here, you need solid nourishment, or you might faint. Come, have some chicken and a piece of meat pie. My mother made them and she is a fabulous cook."

"Thank you a lot, but I won't eat your food that is just for you. Tomorrow I'll bring some more, I promise. For today this will be enough for me."

"I don't insist because I can feel that you start being embarrassed and I don't want that. Let's finish and go back to work."

The four rooms she had to clean were ready by the time of leaving. Lara even found small tips that made her feel better. Close to five o'clock, she was ready to go and take Adam home. By the entrance, she saw the unpleasant woman who inspired her scare since the first moment she saw her.

"Good night Mrs. Wilson", she said, and went outside without waiting any answer.

After she left, Mrs. Wilson called Martha who was about to leave.

"How is she?"

"I think she worked before this job", Martha answered.

"She said that she didn't."

"Come, see for yourself."

They both went and checked thoroughly all the rooms cleaned by Lara.

"Spotless everywhere", Mrs. Wilson said. "She is very good. I hope she stays like that. Is she also a good partner to you?"

"Yes, she is very friendly and pleasant, but sometimes without any reason at all, she shows a sudden fright like she has some trouble in her mind. I don't ask because she is not very talkative. I think she is a very good person."

"Then we'll keep her for the time being. Good night Martha."

In the meantime, Lara walked slowly down the street, trying not to scream of so much pain she felt in her body. Adam was waiting for her with impatience.

"How was your first day on the job?"

"I'll tell you when we get home. Now let's stop by the store and buy a lunch box. My partner said that I should bring more food if I want to last longer on that job."

Once home, Lara said:

"Before dinner, I'll take a hot, very hot shower, and then after we'll eat and talk. My entire body stinks of so much cleaning stuff I had to use and I feel like my bones are melting."

"I'll set the table and warm up the food. Take your time. I'm not very hungry."

She came out of the shower more refreshed and in a much better shape. They talked a lot over dinner and Adam asked her to tell him all the details about the job.

She told him only what she considered that will not make him sad. She asked about his day.

"We learned some simple instructions about computer, but I already knew everything Miss Vanessa taught us. You know something? I miss a lot my room from back home, and mostly my computer."

"I miss my computer also, but you see, we are not allowed to have one connected to the internet by disclosing our address that might let someone to find us. We can have one just to read educational articles, make research, and for playing games. We are not supposed to subscribe to publications or using the email. If you promise to do just that, I can buy a laptop that we can share."

Adam jumped in her arms and kissed her both cheeks:

"I promise and I'll not disappoint you. I know very well the danger that might occur."

"Very well, then. Saturday will go shopping for a laptop. I want to tell you something that might please you. I get small tips left by customers, and I would like to share them with you. In this way, you can save a little money for yourself and enjoy it. What do you think?"

"I think that you are the best mother a child can have. There is no other like you. Having my little money for myself will make me feel like having a big treasure."

She caressed his curled hair and kissed him with the entire warmth of her heart.

Next day when coming home, Diana was outside in front of the door, moping the walk side.

"I spoke with my sister today", she said, "and she told me that you are a very good worker, with good behavior, and she is happy to have you there. She also said that you and Martha make a very good team."

"Thank you Diana for the appreciation. I'm very pleased with my work and talking about Martha, I must say that she is a wonderful person and I like her a lot."

Back to the apartment, Lara said to Adam:

"Today I only had four rooms to clean and feel less tired than yesterday. I'm a little upset though, because my boss said that Saturday I have to work half shift from eight to twelve, and this means that we only can go shopping for the laptop after I finish my job, and in the meantime, you have to stay home alone. The good part is that she we'll pay me double. Are you going to be all right?"

"Nothing to worry about. I'll be fine, reading a book, or watching television. I'm very happy about what Mrs. Diana told you. The only thing I don't like is that you are so tired and look weak when you come back from work."

"I'll get use to it, eat more, sleep better, and get stronger. Let's have dinner and you tell me about your day."

She didn't want to worry him, but she barely could stand on her feet, asking herself for how long she will be able to do that work.

Saturday was already there, Lara went to work, but there was no empty room to clean and she only kept herself busy in the supply room. Close to noon, Martha came and replaced her for the rest of the day.

Shopping was one of Adam's greatest pleasures. It took them quite a long time until they found the laptop they both liked. In that evening they kept busy with connecting to the internet and doing research about what they liked the most. Lots of information was there for both mother and son, giving them the enjoyment missed for a long time. Late evening they went to bed trying to get some sleep, and thinking that next day was Sunday and they both will share time using that new treasure all day long.

One week went by, with hopes for a better and more secure life. By Friday, Mrs. Wilson called Lara and said:

"Your trial period expired, and you'll have permanent position with an increase in your salary. You showed to be a good and reliable worker. Now go back to work, and no need to thank me."

Lara opened her mouth to say something, but the unpleasant woman made her a sign to leave.

In that evening, Adam suggested a celebration for Lara's promotion, but none of them could find how to enjoy the event, other than staying home, and doing what they usually did.

After a few days, Martha approached Lara with a proposal:

"How would you like to come with your boy, for dinner to my house, this coming Saturday? I told a lot to my family about you and they want to meet you. What do you say?"

"Thank you for your kindness. I'll be glad to come and meet your family, but your little girl will not be scared seeing my face?"

"Don't you worry about Samantha. I've already told her about your accident and about your face. She will not be scared at all. Besides, she will enjoy a lot the company of Adam. Saturday at five, I'll be in front of your building and we'll drive to my home, which is about half hour far from here."

Adam was thrilled by that new adventure when she told him. It was a long time since he didn't experience anything exiting to get him out of the ordinary.

"Listen, and pay attention to what I'm telling you", his mother said. "Those people certainly will ask questions about us, and I'll have to swim in a pool of lies. Don't try to jump in and rescue me. Don't open your mouth, stay quiet, and don't even blink. You know well how hard is for me to tell lies, but you also know that I have to, when it comes to our particular situation."

"Don't worry. I know very well, and I promise to be good and behave properly."

"Before, we'll go shopping for something nice, like a present for Martha's mother and for Samantha, her little girl and maybe a bottle of expensive wine for Mr. Jessie Davies, her husband."

In the coming Saturday at five o'clock they were in front of the main door, when only in few minutes Martha showed up.

"You better be hungry," she said, "because my mother always cooks like for a battalion. We are almost there."

The car stopped in front of a nice house surrounded by a very well groomed flower garden. Mrs. Rose Taylor, Martha's mother showed at the door, accompanied by Jessie and Samantha. They shook hands with the guests and invited them inside, and no one showed any sign of disgust or scare by looking at Lara's face.

"Welcome to our home", Rose said, "and thank you for the presents. Come, and have a seat until dinner is served."

The house was not very large, but very neat and nicely furnished. A casual conversation looked to be very comfortable for Lara and seemingly no less for the hosts. The food was indeed incredibly tasty and served in huge portions. It was a very pleasant atmosphere, like among friends, when Rose addressed Lara:

"Where are you from?"

"Parker, Arizona, a small town on the Colorado River, with only about four thousand people."

"Martha told us that you're a widow. How did you manage to make a living and support your child?", Jessie asked.

"My husband died little after Adam was born and I made a pretty good living for both, working as a seamstress in a dry cleaner shop. There I had an accident caused by a drying machine, and after that, I worked at home. Not long after, I decided to move to a bigger city where I could find a job and there will be more opportunities for Adam to attend a good school and grow up in better conditions."

"You had a hard life", Rose said, "but looks like you did pretty well. You must be proud of yourself."

"I'm trying to do what I think is best for us, and I cannot complain."

She felt that a few more questions would make her collapse. Seemingly, everybody was satisfied with her explanations because no one asked her anything anymore. Drinks and coffee were served in the living room, while Samantha kept Adam busy, showing him her room and her toys. It was time to go home.

After a warm handshake, and before leaving, they promised to see each others again. Martha drove them home and embraced them both.

"It was so good for you to come and meet my family. They all liked you both a lot", she said.

"They are the nicest people I've met in a very long time. Thank you Martha for being such a good friend and inviting us. I'll see you Monday."

It was quite late when they entered the apartment.

"You can breathe now", Adam said, showing a beautiful smile and a lot of warmth to his mother.

"Are you making fun of me? A few more questions had they asked, and I would have run out of answers."

"You did so well, that even I who became master of lies couldn't have done better. Now tell me what a seamstress is?"

"Someone whose occupation is sewing and I must

tell you that I don't know much about this craft. Let's go to sleep now."

By the middle of the next week, while Lara was doing her job, she heard a lot of noise in the room next door. A couple who just checked in, started fighting, screaming, and breaking the furniture. Lara rushed to see Martha who worked at the end of the corridor and told her about the incident.

"I'll go to the office to see Mrs. Wilson and call the police. You go to the supply room, lock yourself inside, and stay there until I'll come and let you out."

She rushed to the office and Lara ran to the supply room and did what Martha asked her to do.

"Is she suspecting something?", Lara asked herself. "How did she manage to suspect me of hiding the truth, and what does she think the truth might be? I wished I could tell her, but I cannot."

She remembered exactly the words said by that woman who had an uneven step and walked with a limp, and who questioned her in that night in the shelter: "Don't trust anybody, no matter how good or friendly someone might be. One time or the other that person could utter a misplaced word and you can end up dead."

After a little while, Martha was at the door:

"You can come out now. That couple made lot of trouble and the police arrested them. You cannot clean that room until the furniture will be replaced. They smashed lots of things and made a real mess. You can go back now, and resume your work. And also, Lara, I have to tell you that I wasn't born yesterday."

Lara thought that indeed, Martha suspected the truth, but didn't ask any question. She just felt sad by being unable to share her secret with that wonderful woman.

The month of March went by. Lara and Adam had a smooth life, feeling quite safe, and being surrounded by people who were friendly and showed no curiosity about their way of existence, when one day a calamity happened. It was already the month of April when one Friday evening, Diana showed up at the door. She was shaking and looked very disturbed. Lara let her in and asked what happened.

"Did you see on TV? Yours and Adam's pictures are posted as fugitives and the authorities are looking for you."

Lara stopped breathing and stood there without moving. She turned on the television and indeed, there was her picture showing the beauty she used to be and Adam's photo from one year ago. The report said that she was a fugitive who abducted her son, and people who saw her are asked to report to the police, because her distressed husband wanted to have his son back.

"What are you going to do?", Diana asked.

"I have to pack up our things and find another place to hide. If he finds us, he will kill me and he will throw Adam on the street."

Adam was nearby and heard what his mother just said.

"I saw our pictures also, and I'll help packing. Let's go Mom, and find a place where he cannot find us."

"We'll go to the railroad station and take the first train heading East. Diana, you have been a good friend and we both thank you for everything you did for us. I'm sorry that I have to leave without saying goodbye to Mrs. Wilson and Martha. Besides, I could use a reference letter to help me find a job, but there is no time to ask."

"My sister and I, we own both buildings and I'll give you the reference you need. I'll be back in a minute."

Diana left and both Lara and Adam started to pack their belongings, leaving out everything that didn't fit in two suitcases. It was already Saturday early morning, and they were ready to go, when a police officer showed up downstairs at Diana's door. He showed her the pictures and asked for the apartment. How did the police find them it was a question mark for everybody. Diana understood that there was no way to hide any longer the two fugitives and went upstairs with the officer. Lara opened the door, giving up all hopes to run away.

"Are you Andrea Benson?", the officer asked.

"Yes, I am."

"This is your son, Justin Benson?"

"Yes, he is."

"You are wanted by the authorities for abducting the son of Marc Benson, and you have to come with me to the police station for questioning. The boy will come with you."

"I'm coming with them", Diana said, "just in case the boy needs help. I'll follow you with my car."

At the police station, they were asked to have a seat

and wait. After about half hour, an officer escorted Lara to the captain bureau. He was probably in his early fifties, his hair was all white, and his eyes had a piercing look.

"Let the boy in", the captain told the officer, and then he addressed Lara:

"Andrea Benson, you are a fugitive and you are accused by your husband for kidnapping his son. What do you have to say?"

"Nothing, because my face tells you all."

"You know that you can go to prison for many years, and lose your son forever?"

"I know very well the law, and what perspectives are for me in the future. Nevertheless, I took my chances and tried to have a safe life for myself and especially for my son. I failed."

He took a long look at her and at Adam, made a long pause and said:

"You are free to go, Andrea. I will not let a monster to find you and have the boy back. Go far to the East, find a big city, and keep a low profile for the time being. The laws in those parts are more clement regarding cases like yours."

Lara was stunned. She couldn't move or utter a word. She opened her mouth but no sound came out. Adam came close to the captain, and gently touched his hand:

"You are good to us, Sir. You did justice for us. If my father finds us he will kill my mother and he will throw me on the street. (He just remembered the words his mother told Diana) You saved my mother's life and mine."

The captain caressed his head and said with an almost imperceptible tremble in his voice:

"You'll make a fine lawyer when you'll grow up. Go now, and take good care of your mother."

He didn't wait for any word coming from Lara, made a sign to the officer standing by to escort them outside and started writing. He barely could hear Lara's whisper:

"Thank you Sir, from all my heart."

Outside, Diana saw them both smiling and she understood instantly that everything went surprisingly good for them. She embraced both and they rushed to her car.

"The captain let us free to go", Lara said. "I have to pinch myself to make sure that I'm not dreaming. He said to go far East and find a big city where it would be easier for us to hide for the time being. I thought that maybe Boston is far from here and a good place for us to start. We had packed already our belongings and we can take the train tonight. What do you think, Diana?"

"As much as I'll miss you both, I think that such a chance will not come twice. Let's go home, take your luggage and I'll drive you to the railroad station. Here is your reference paper."

Before going home, they stopped by the bank and Lara took all her money from the safe deposit box, and closed the account.

It was around six o'clock evening when they arrived

to the station. The next train to Boston was scheduled for departure around seven o'clock. Lara bought two tickets for a roomette, since there will be more comfortable for them to sleep in a bed and have a good rest. Little before boarding the train, they embraced Diana who started crying, showing a big sadness to see them go.

The ticket controller signed all the passengers to board the train, and mentioned to every one the seat and the direction of the compartment.

In a roomette, daytime seating converts to beds at night. It is provided with in-room toilet and sink, and electrical outlets, climate controls, reading lights, a small closet and a fold-down table are all within easy reach. Also, the passengers are entitled to receive all regular meals as part of their accommodations. That meant full breakfast, lunch and dinner.

Lara and Adam entered their compartment, and the train started moving after few minutes.

"Are you hungry?", Lara asked. "We have not eaten since yesterday."

"A little, but rather I like to have some sleep."

There was a knock at the door, and a young man showed up.

"Good evening", he said, "my name is John and I'm the steward for this car at your service for the entire journey. Would you like me to do the beds?"

"Yes, please. Nice meeting you, John", Lara said.

He made the beds and before leaving, he added:

"I strongly suggest that you use the seatbelts for the upper bed. If you need anything else, please press this button and I'll be glad to help. Breakfast is served in the dining car which is next on your right, between seven and nine."

"I rather would prefer to have all our meals here, instead of going to the dining car, if it's not too much trouble", Lara said.

"Not at all. Here is the menu, check on the list what you like and I'll be glad to place the order and bring it to you."

Lara chose a hearty breakfast, mentioning that eight o'clock will be the right time, and saying that for the other meals they will talk tomorrow. Adam was asleep in a corner; she took him in her arms, dressed him for the night, and let him sleep on the lower bed, securing him with the seatbelts. She lay on the upper bed trying without any success to get some sleep. Her thoughts were swirling in her mind bringing on the surface many memories dear to her. It was not a single day passing without her remembering her parents. They both were kind and considerate, with great regard for other people's feelings, never misjudging them for their behavior. They both were school teachers and gave Andrea a sturdy education with French and piano lessons, pursuing their highest wish to give her the opportunity to achieve a brilliant career. She remembered their soft voices when they both told her stories about life and people they knew and had a cultural impact on their lives when they were young. When they died, Andrea was devastated. She not only lost her parents, but also the best friends she ever had.

The teachings they left her became a treasure that always remained dear to her and helped her to overcome many times the hardship she was compelled to encounter.

She remembered how proud she always was of everything she achieved in her life. She was successful in school, in work, in being a mother, and in being a friend. She made with care and joy the path of her life that was supposed to be smooth and secure forever. Her relationship with people was situated on the highest level of respect, admiration, and esteem. She was rewarded for her mind, for her work, for her reputation, and for her behavior. Her unusual beauty was highly admired, and she was aware of it; people used to turn their heads when she walked by, just to have a glimpse of her. No less, her capability of sustaining an intellectual discussion was a delightful pleasure for people in her league. One day came, though, when she was compelled to beg not only for her rights, but also for her life, and for the life of her child. People started to treat her with pity and condescendence raised from the sorrow evoked by her suffering, distress, and misfortune. Now, she lost her pride, her dignity, and her self-esteem, being forced to bow her head before everybody and to accept a state of humility just to preserve what was left of her wounded soul. With all her badly hurt feelings, she only could find in her soul a tiny grain of courage to make one-step at a time, to fight for her life and for the life of her child.

With these thoughts in her mind, and with heavy tears in her eyes, Lara fell asleep.

Adam woke up before her and touched her arm. Lara opened her eyes and smile at him:

"How did you sleep?", she asked. "Are you hungry? I'll be up in a minute."

"I don't know how I got in the bed, but I slept like a baby, and I'm terribly hungry."

"The steward will be here shortly and he will bring us the breakfast. I ordered a huge one. There he is."

John was at the door handling a big tray.

"Good morning, Madame. I hope you had a good rest; the young gentleman must be very hungry."

"Good morning, John. This is my son, Adam, and indeed he is famished, the same as I am."

"Hi John, I'm pleased to meet you. After breakfast, I'll enjoy better this journey."

John smiled at him, converted the beds to seats, and left after taking their order for lunch and dinner. Before leaving, Lara asked him for newspapers, maps, and guides. She also asked about the point where the train was by that time.

"We are close to San Antonio, Texas, which will be followed by Austin and Dallas. You have everything here in this pouch", he said, "even if the newspapers are a few days old."

The landscape outside was beautiful. They even spotted a small waterfall and a woman riding a horse. Even if it was cold weather, people enjoyed a good time in front of their houses. It was a wonderful scenery going from ground level all the way to the far hills covered with snow.

"I have to look into this papers and maps; maybe I could find some information about housing and a job. In the meantime, you keep yourself busy with the laptop or with whatever you like. It would be a good idea if you resume your French lessons. Search the internet for short stories written in French for children and read them loud, so that I can hear you. We are not supposed to go outside this compartment, and that's why we'll have our meals here."

"I'll look through the window for a while, and then I'll look for stories, or I'll join you in hunting for whatever we need."

After few minutes she heard him reading a story called *"Les meilleurs amis du monde"*. Lara interrupted her search and paid attention to him. It was music to her ears, and a real delight to listen what a beautiful French accent he had. After half hour, he finished the story and his face showed a big satisfaction.

"Well?", he asked. "Did you like the story of '*Nestor le canard*'? I found a very good site with French stories."

"I must say that I'm impressed and very proud of you. Bookmark the page and you will be able to read more stories. I worked hard on your accent, and I have to say that we both are rewarded. Keep reading and also, we can talk in French from time to time."

"Did you find what you were looking for?"

"I found some very interesting stuff, like a luxurious hotel, twelve stories, and a penthouse, which also has a daycare facility. Nearby, there is a building with furnished apartments for rent which will suits us very well. We can follow the same plan as we had before, and we should hope for the best."

"I'm hoping that everything will be all right for us. Look outside! The ground is all covered with snow!"

The train headed north and approached Chicago, the temperature was decreasing, and the snow level was noticeably rising. Next day, they arrived to Boston with a short delay. John helped them with the luggage, got a big tip for his service, and a warm hug.

A cab took them to a nearby motel when it was almost evening, and the first thing Lara did, was to turn on the television. There were no pictures of them and no threats from the police looking for them.

"Tomorrow I'll go to find a job, and you'll stay here and wait for me. You have enough things to entertain yourself and not getting bored. We have enough food from the train and I'll buy more on my way back. Is this acceptable?"

"Don't worry about me. I know exactly what I am supposed to do, and you can be sure that I'll be all right."

Next morning, Lara took the bus and went to the address of the hotel. It was indeed huge, very elegant, had a casino, and a health club featuring an indoor pool under a retractable glass roof.

In the guide she studied, it was described as being close to art galleries, sidewalk cafés, and cozy neighborhoods to explore. In addition, it was not far away from the Boston Public Library, the ever-popular Copley Square, Trinity Church, and the Prudential Center. She asked a clerk at the desk for the supervisor of the personal team who worked as housekeepers. A short woman probably in her forties showed up with some kind of wonder in her eyes, and raised her eyebrows when she saw Lara's face.

"You asked for me? What can I do for you?"

"My name is Lara Collins, I came last night from Phoenix, I have a six years old son, and I badly need a place to work. I am a good housekeeper and know very well how to do my job."

"We only hire here people who are referred to us. Do you have any references?"

"Yes, I have. Here is the letter of reference given to me by my supervisor from the last place where I worked."

Lara gave her the sealed envelope with the letter written by Diana. She never read it because she was sure that if the envelope was sealed it would show more confidence. The woman opened the envelope and read the letter a few times.

"If you are as good as she describes you, than you'll have the job, but first on a trial period of one week. If I'm satisfied with your work, I'll give you the permanent position. Your son can stay in our daycare facility while you will be working. You'll start tomorrow, your shift is from eight to five, and be here before. At the front desk, you'll find all the instructions to follow. My name is Greta Dietrich."

"Thank you Mrs. Dietrich, from the bottom of my heart. I promise not to disappoint you."

Lara made a big effort not to jump and kiss her. Outside on the street, she almost cried of so much joy. She rushed back to the motel and told Adam everything about the interview.

"You don't know how happy I am for both of us", he said. "Now we need a place to stay. When are we going to look for one?"

"We can start today. I found a couple of addresses and we can go and see. Would you like us to do just that?"

"Let's not waste any time, Mom!"

Lara asked the clerk downstairs for directions, they took a bus and arrived at the corner of the street. After walking a short distance, they arrived in front of a four stories building with the sign for rent in front of the door. A nice woman was at the desk; she seemed not to notice Lara's face, and she was pleased to show them a one-bedroom apartment at the third floor, all furnished and quite elegant. Lara had no second thoughts; she paid the rent for the first month, and said that they will be back with their luggage by the end of the day. It was already late afternoon when they returned to the motel, took their belongings, and went to their new home. On the way there, a small store was nearby; they entered and bought a lot of food supply, to last for the rest of the week.

First thing they did when inside the apartment, they embraced each other and started dancing. Seemingly, the good Providence decided to be on their side, for a change.

"Tomorrow after work we go to the bank, and after that we go to buy everything we need for our household", Lara said. "Too bad that we couldn't take the many things we had in Phoenix."

Early in the morning, they were ready to go. Their new home was only two blocks away from the hotel, and the bus at the corner of the street took them there in only a few minutes. At the front desk, Lara found all the instructions left for her by Mrs. Dietrich. First, she followed the directions to the daycare facility, which was located at the end of a labyrinth of long corridors. Mrs. Dietrich already notified the Director about the newcomers; he welcomed Adam with kindness, asked him a lot of questions, and gave Lara all the information she needed.

After walking back those long corridors and many others alike, finally Lara arrived at the office of Greta Dietrich. She signed some papers, got a uniform, and started the tour of the house to get familiar with her new surroundings. It had twelve floors, about four hundred rooms, and the upper two floors were designed only as suites. On top of everything was a huge penthouse.

"You will start cleaning the ten rooms on the eight floor which are located on the East side; do as many as you can. At the edge of the corridor, you'll find the supply room with all you need to do your job. You can ask any housekeeper on the floor to show you how to start your work, or for anything else, you need. You have one-hour break for lunch in the housekeeping quarter; you can buy your meal or you can bring it from home. Before finishing your shift call me at this number and I'll come up to inspect your work."

She turned around and left. Lara didn't waste any minute, followed the instructions, and started cleaning the first of the ten rooms she was supposed to do in that day. It was a real mess, and the others were the same. She thought that the motel of Mrs. Wilson was a toy compared to this hotel. By lunchtime, she almost finished six rooms, but felt tired, thinking that she needed all her available energy to finish the rest. The lunchroom was crowded with all the housekeepers who came in groups or alone, but none paid attention to her. Later she found out that because of the hard job and Mrs. Dietrich's demands, not many of them lasted too long in that place. Lara thought that nobody makes friends there. All together, there were about sixty housekeepers who made that hotel to be one of the best in town.

She bought something to eat and went back to work before the break time was over. She managed to finish cleaning all the rooms, and called Mrs. Dietrich before leaving. In that day, she got big tips left by the customers who left, and she thought that Adam would be very pleased with his share. Mrs. Dietrich checked thoroughly all the rooms from wall to wall and each corner without missing a spot.

"Starting tomorrow, you'll clean the first five suites on the floor above, starting from the East corner. This will be your new assignment, from now on. You can leave now."

She turned around and left. Lara rushed to the daycare to pick up Adam, and both went to the bank, opened an account, and secured the cash they still have in to a deposit box. After that, they went shopping everything they needed for the household, and didn't forget to buy a cell phone for each. Both were eager to tell their story of the day, but decided to talk about everything when they get back home. With lots of packages and boxes, they took a cab and arrived there late evening. While arranging everything they bought in the right place, they talked a lot about their day. Lara almost forgot how tired she felt before, and joined her son in his big excitement.

"I like a lot my new daycare center", he said. "There are three classes ordered by age, and one special for the babies. In my class, we are about twenty-seven children and Miss Sarah is very nice and very friendly. She tested my level of knowledge and said that I'm very bright. Only three of my classmates can read and write. She asked me to tell a story in front of the class and was very pleased, because the children paid a lot of attention to what I narrated, and that was the story of Jack, the boy who was lost in the woods, and Amber the deer helped him to find his way home. Tomorrow she will take us to the Park Zoo, and I'm very excited. Now, tell me about your day."

Lara told him everything about her day, except that there were moments when she couldn't feel her body.

Her impression was that moving to the upper floor meant a promotion and a permanent job.

"I'm very, and I mean very happy for you and for me too. I like it here a lot and I hope we can stay here and have a good life. Don't you think so, Mom?"

"I only can hope, but I must say that this is a good place for us. Here is your share of the tips. Where do you keep your money?"

"Wow! This is big! I keep it in the nightstand and count it every day."

"Maybe we should ask and open an account with the bank in your name. You will be able to save money that you might use later. Now let's eat and then go to sleep."

Next day Lara started her new assignment. First, she checked every suite and was shocked by the filth inside.

"Rich people are the dirtiest creatures on this planet", she said to herself. "They allow themselves to despise the work of those who work hard for their existence. If I don't die today of exhaustion, I might never die, at all."

Lara started to clean the first suite, and in that day, she gave up her lunch break. By the end of her shift she barely could move. Mrs. Dietrich came over and checked every suite in every corner and every spot.

"I shortened your period of trial; you have a permanent job with increase of pay. I never said this to any of my employees, but I must admit that your work is above my expectations."

She turned around and left, without waiting for Lara to thank her.

Back home, Lara told Adam about their new perspective to improve their lives. She looked very tired and barely touched the food.

"Your hands are all red and swollen, and you smell bad", Adam said. "You might get sick and I don't want any improvement in our lives at this price."

"It won't be every day for me to clean all five suites since they will not be vacated all at the same time. I'll be fine, and don't worry. How was your day?"

"Didn't do much. Everything was exciting in the beginning when I first attended the program of the daycare. Now it's becoming boring. Miss Sarah teaches us how to read and write and some computing with numbers from one to ten. I would like to learn things that I don't know and are interesting for me."

"For the time being, we cannot do anything about, because of my work and my schedule. You have to take the situation just the way it is, have patience, and wait for the month of September when you'll start the school. Nevertheless, I am thinking that in the meantime, you should learn online the curriculum for the first and second grade, and at the beginning of the school year, we should apply for you to attend the third grade. For this, you'll have to be tested and if you pass, you'll be enrolled directly in to the third grade, and skip from the beginning all the boring material. You'll be happy to learn many new and exciting subjects. What do you think?"

"I'm thrilled! Can we do this, Mom?"

"At least we can try, but I'm pretty sure that we can have the approval of the school for you to take the test. Start today; you have four months till then and I'm always here to help you."

By the end of the week, while she was ready to leave, Mrs. Dietrich showed up.

"The owner of this hotel is Mrs. Patricia Jenkins who also owns two big apartment buildings located in the historic heart of Boston near the Faneuil Hall Market Place, and some other properties in the suburbs. She is extremely rich. Every month she comes here for the Casino, and stays upstairs in the penthouse for about three days. Your new assignment besides the suites is to be at her services for the time she will stay here. You will be day and night, around her, answering to all her requests, no matter how strange they might be. She will come tomorrow morning around ten, but before that, I'll show you the place and tell you what your duties will be. You will get extra pay and three free meals a day. Do you have any questions?"

"Just one. What am I supposed to do with my child, since under no circumstances I cannot leave him home alone?"

"The daycare is open twenty-four hours, seven days a week. Your child will be in very good hands and I'll talk in this regard to the employee in charge. You can see him at anytime when Mrs. Jenkins will be busy in the Casino. Anything else?"

"No, Mrs. Dietrich. I'll be here at eight tomorrow morning."

On the way home, Lara told Adam about their new annoyance. In the last few months, they learned how to handle hardship and much frustration only by being close to each other, by sharing their thoughts, and by taking decisions together. The bond between them was indestructible.

Next morning, Mrs. Dietrich showed her the penthouse. It was huge and occupied almost the whole floor with a view of the city all the way to the ocean. It had an apartment-like ambiance, with French doors separating the oversize living room and spacious bedrooms. It had an electric-burning fireplace, vintage crystal chandelier, an Italian marble bathroom, and classic furnishings. Lara never saw such luxury in her entire life.

"It's breathtaking", she said."

"This place has to be spotless at all time she stays here. Take a piece of paper and write down everything I tell you. She might stay here three days and three nights. In the first day, the bed sheets are of pink color, and so are the towels and the bathrobe. The next day, they all are of green color, and the day to come they must be all of blue color. The soap in the first day will be of lavender scent, the next day will be lilac, and the following day will be jasmine. You will help her with a bubble bath and a body massage that she takes whenever she feels like. You also will help her with the dresses and shoes she will choose to wear. Whenever she calls you, be quick and don't waste your time. The butler, Paul, is assigned to serve her drinks and meals. She might use a language that will be improper and might offend you; don't pay attention to it because this is the way she treats everybody who is not a member of her club. She might also fire you, for no reason at all; if she does, don't worry, because your place on the floor below is always yours. If you encounter any difficulty in doing your job, call me. I know her for a very long time. The supply room is at the end of the hall; there is a bed at your convenience for the night and for breaks during the day where you can rest. Now, I leave you alone; she will be here in about half hour, greet her, state your name and help her unpacking the luggage.

"I'll do my best", Lara said.

By ten o'clock, the door opened and Mrs. Jenkins entered like a storm, followed by Paul who carried no less than four suitcases. She was quite a slightly chubby woman, of medium height, good looking, very well dressed, apparently in her forties.

"Good morning, Madame", Lara said, "my name is Lara, I am your maid, at Madame's service."

"Where the hell do you come from, with this ugly face? Where is the other one?", the tempestuous woman asked and started to throw things around.

"I don't know, Madame. I am assigned to be at your service", Lara said with a soft voice and a contemptuous look in her eyes.

The woman called on the phone Mrs. Dietrich who showed up and asked her what she wanted.

"Greta, who is this ugly creature, and where is the other one?"

"Patricia, you fired her, and this is your new maid at your service." She addressed Lara: "Give us a minute, please."

Lara stepped outside, closing the door and covering her years. The two women started shouting at each other like in hell. After a few minutes, Lara was called inside, and Mrs. Dietrich said:

"Do the unpacking, Lara, and then follow the instructions I gave you."

She left, and Lara started unpacking without saying a word. She arranged everything in the closet, showing a lot of ability in what she was doing, while the stormy woman watched every move she made.

"Make me a drink", she said.

"Madame has to ask Paul. He is the butler and he will serve you the drink. I'm the maid and I am supposed to do only my job."

Mrs. Jenkins looked furious, but tried to temper her voice when she said:

"You are not only very ugly, but also very impertinent. Call Paul."

The butler came in and made her a drink. He was assigned to escort her everywhere she went for the entire period of her stay.

"I'll be back at three", she said and left with Paul.

Lara knew from Mrs. Dietrich the entire schedule. She went to the casino to play roulette until close to three, after which she will come up for a nap, until about five, and then she will go back to the casino and play bridge until one o'clock at night. Before going to bed, she will take a bubble bath for about one hour. After she left in that morning, Lara cleaned the place, making everything shining, and then rushed downstairs to see Adam. His face radiated with joy when he saw his mother, and asked her in French, such as not to be heard by the others:

"How did you manage to sneak out?"

"It's a long story, and I'll tell you all about when we'll get home. Are you comfortable by spending here so much time, day and night?"

"I'll be all right. I'll be staying at night with two more kids. Miss Sarah will be replaced with someone else by the end of her shift, but you don't have to worry about. What are you going to do?"

"I have a bed in a nearby room, and three meals that will be brought to me. It's not bad, but I miss you and our home doing things together. We have to talk a lot about that test and find all the information we need, such that you can meet all the requirements. We'll work together one-step at the time to make sure you pass the test successfully. Are you still convinced that you want it?"

"More than ever. I thought carefully about being in third grade at my age, and finishing school sooner. Yes, Mom, I want to pass successfully that test."

Lara kissed his cheeks with all her love.

"I must go now. If you need me, and this is only in extreme case, call me on my cell but only texting.

If I can, I'll come to see you in the afternoon. If not, we'll see each other tomorrow morning. Your French is superb. Bye, my dearest."

Lara went upstairs, waiting for Mrs. Jenkins to come back from her roulette gambling. It was past lunchtime and in the supply room, she found a tray with her meal, which was already cold. She looked for a piece of cloth and covered her face, living only her eyes to be noticed.

It was about three o'clock when Mrs. Jenkins escorted by Paul, returned to the penthouse. Lara was next to the bed, holding the house robe and the slippers, and helped her to change clothes.

"Why did you cover your face?"

"To make Madame more comfortable."

The stormy woman said nothing, but she felt like being slapped on her face by that very neat servant who seemed to be very well trained to do an excellent job. Lara smiled under her cover and knew exactly what a humiliation that woman felt. She helped her to bed, covered her with the comforter, pulled the window curtains to shut out the light from the outside, and left. On her way out, she talked to herself with a low voice:

"*Elle n'est pas vraiment si folle que je pensais.*"

Paul was outside and he heard her.

"*Parlez-vous français?*"

"*Un peu.*"

They both looked at each other with big contentment, like two old friends who knew each other for long time, and continued talking in French. Paul and his wife came to the States many years ago on vacation, they both liked Boston, and decided to stay and have a good life here. Lara told him as little as she could about herself and her son, but he didn't ask any additional questions. He was surprised by her Parisian accent and by her fluency in French, but didn't look for details. They talked about many pleasant subjects until Mrs. Jenkins' awakening time.

The bell rang and they both rushed to the door.

Paul gave her the drink, and Lara helped her with the dress and shoes she chose from the wardrobe. Around five, she was ready to leave, escorted by Paul. Ana whispered to her new friend:

"Before coming back, please give me a call so I can prepare her bath in time."

They left and she knew that they will be back around one o'clock and not earlier. Lara didn't waste a minute more, and rushed downstairs to see Adam. He was playing some games on the computer, talking to one of his classmates.

"I'm so happy to see you!", he shouted, and with a lower voice, he said, "I'm bored already with this games and I'm not allowed to search for something interesting. How was your day since we saw each other this morning?"

"It was not bad at all, but I'm worried about you. We still have to go one day and two nights with this schedule, and then we go home and feel much better. Can you resist until then without being annoyed?"

"Yes, I believe so. I forgot to tell you that we are going to start Monday a workout program to do gymnastics and play ball. I think this is awesome, since I feel that I need to move around and have some physical activity."

"Marvelous! I think you'll enjoy a lot the program."

The employee for the night shift was an older woman by the name Wanda. Lara saw her and said:

"May I stay a little longer with my son? My name is Lara; I work at the penthouse and now is my break time."

"Stay as long as you want, Lara, until he goes to bed. Adam is a very nice and a very bright boy. He knows a lot of stories, he tells them to the other children and helps me a lot, because I ran out of imagination."

Other three children joined them and Lara was pleased to answer to the many questions they had. In that evening, she told them stories, some real, some invented, and the children including Adam enjoyed a lot her company. It was already time for her to leave.

"Are you coming tomorrow morning?", Adam asked.

"I'll be here in the afternoon, and we'll talk as usually. Until then you have a good night sleep, and later I'll try to have mine."

They embraced each other, and Lara went back to the penthouse. She checked the entire place to make sure that everything was in order, then she took a book from the living room, and went to the supply room. She was asleep when the phone rang around one o'clock, and Paul said that they were on the way up. Lara rushed to prepare the bath just in time. Mrs. Jenkins was in a terrible mood, but that was her usual way of behaving, and didn't impress Lara at all. She helped her with the bath, gave her a good massage, and put her to bed. Before leaving, Lara turned off all the lights and asked her if she needed anything else.

"Go away! I'm too tired to need anything, especially you!"

Lara had a contemptuous smile knowing exactly why she couldn't throw more insolence at her. No matter how weird that woman was, she had to accept that Lara's service was without reproach.

The next morning, Mrs. Jenkins woke up at ten, and the day was the same as the one before. Monday was already there, Lara made her luggage, and Mrs. Jenkins left around ten in the morning, without saying a word. Lara started cleaning thoroughly every corner and spot, when she saw a hundred dollar bill on top of the dresser.

"Probably she won it last night and misplaced it", she said to herself. I'll give it to Mrs. Dietrich."

After finishing her job, she went downstairs and told Mrs. Dietrich about the money, giving it to her.

"She never misplaces money. This is the tip she left for you. Don't be surprised, because she is always unpredictable. Take the rest of the day off, and tomorrow return to the suites."

Lara rushed to the daycare to take Adam home. He just came back from the gym program and was very excited.

"It's incredibly invigorating! I feel so much more energetic, and I like it a lot!"

Lara kissed him and said that she had the rest of the

day off and came to take him home. She reserved the surprise of the money for later.

"What would you like us to do? We can go for a walk in downtown, or go shopping, or go home."

"Let's do all of the above", Adam answered.

"I have an idea", Lara said. "We walk to the bookstore, and buy some books, mostly for you to learn for the test. Every weekend and maybe half hour every evening, we are going to do together some homework, following the curriculum for the first and second grade. It will be easier for you to learn from books than from the internet. What do you think?"

"Let's go and see what we can find. I know already what books I need, since I search online."

They had a long walk to the main bookstore in downtown. It had all the book sections one can imagine. They found everything for Adam, and some books for Lara. A mid sized world globe completed a big package with educational material, to be not only studied, but also greatly enjoyed.

Once arrived home, they put everything in the right places and Lara said that before dinner they had to shower first since they both were away from home for already three days and couldn't take much care of themselves. The meal she cooked in that evening was highly appreciated, especially that a good, long conversation supplemented an atmosphere of warm feelings and understanding.

"There is much beauty in this world, and there is much ugliness", Lara said. "Try to see and understand both sides and judge everything with fairness. Try to reach the human mind where knowledge resides and no matter how much you know, there is always someone above you, and someone below. Try to reach the mind and soul of that one who is above you. Try to learn as much as you can, because knowledge is the most delightful and rewarding pleasure a human being can have."

"I will never forget what you just said."

He jumped into her arms and kissed her both disfigured cheeks.

"Let's talk about something gratifying for the time being. How much money do you have?", Lara asked.

"Almost one hundred."

"Well, today you'll add fifty more, since I got one hundred as a tip from Mrs. Jenkins."

"This is awesome! I'm rich! You said she doesn't like you too much."

"Seemingly, she changed her opinion, and she started liking me. How would you like to open a saving account with a bank?"

She explained him how that account will work for him at his age; he understood very well what a custodial account meant, and both decided to go to the bank as soon as they'll have time.

Every weekend and half hour every evening, they worked together for the test. It was a lot of material for Adam to absorb, but he enjoyed everything he learned. They both had a tied schedule, but with good planning and an organized system, the result of their work showed the expected success. Lara made a thorough search to find a good school close to home and found one just the way she wanted. She read good reviews about the teachers, sizes of classes, and most of all about the high percentage of students' good performance. It was a school with grades from one to eight; it had also a kinder Care after school program, and was located about two blocks from home. She told Adam everything she found, and a notable detail to take in consideration:

"They offer an optional opportunity for learning a foreign language. If you want, you can choose French, Italian, or German. This is a supplementary hour, twice a week, outside the regular schedule."

"Certainly, I would like to learn either Italian or German, since French I master quite well."

"I'll tell you what you are going to do: You can find a lot of lessons online, to listen and choose the language you like the most. When you decide which one you want to learn, we can ask the Principal to enroll you in the program. Sounds good?"

"Very good. I can't wait."

After many times listening to the samples offered online, he chose German, because he said, "It's a language very much spoken in all the fields of any highly regarded profession".

By the end of July, Adam was well prepared to take the test. Lara examined him thoroughly many times in all the details, making sure that he feels secure and self-confident. The Placement Test had to be taken before enrollment and the last day to submit it was August 3rd.

Lara typed an application in her very academic English, took the day off from work, and they both went to the school. The Principal received them with kindness, asked many questions about Adam's background and the reason he wanted to start school in 3rd grade. Apparently, he was satisfied with all the answers, and scheduled the date for the tests for the next Monday at nine o'clock.

The few days until then, were more relaxing for both of them. Adam mastered the material so well that he did not need to revise it again.

"Are you nervous?", Lara asked.

"No. I'm very confident."

Monday morning they went to school. After a few minutes, the Principal took Adam inside a room where two teachers were sitting in front of a desk. One of them showed him a seat, gave him the writing test, and let him work for half hour. After that, he asked him to read from a book, a short story, and explain some of the words. Finally, the other teacher gave him the math test, with lots of computations and geometrical shapes. Adam had not a bit of hesitation and solved the test ahead of time. He did everything so well, that at the end of examination, both teachers were extremely pleased and the Principal congratulated him and his mother who during all that time was pacing the corridor outside, back and forth.

"Adam, you did great. We'll see you by the first of September, in the 3rd grade. Mrs. Collins, we have here a student with a very bright future. Congratulations to you both."

Once outside, they both jumped and embraced each other of so much joy.

"The tests you gave me at home were much harder than these ones."

"I'm very proud of you. Our joint efforts have been rewarded. We'll celebrate later your success, because now I have to go back to work and you go to daycare."

In that coming weekend, Mrs. Jenkins brought her family to the penthouse. Edgar, her husband was the co-owner of the hotel and he owned also a furniture factory. His biggest passion was to sculpt wood and make artistic pieces of furniture in his workshop at home where he spent a lot of his time. Mr. Jenkins was a very brunet, good looking, attractive man, with not much affection for his wife. He was a couple of years younger than she was, and it seemed they had rather a marriage of convenience and not one of love.

The daughter Suzie was their nine years old girl, very pretty and looking much like her father.

Lara and Paul greeted them when they arrived in that Saturday morning, making sure that every one was comfortable with the accommodations and service.

Mrs. Jenkins said to Suzie with a monotone voice:

"We are going downstairs and you stay here and find something to entertain yourself."

"With Madame's permission may I make a suggestion?", Lara asked.

"Since when servants make me suggestions without being asked?", Mrs. Jenkins jumped like a cat.

Lara kept quiet and was ready to open the deck to give Suzie at least the pleasure of looking over the city, when Mr. Jenkins asked:

"What do you suggest, Lara?"

"With Madame's and Monsieur's permission I'll be glad to escort Miss Suzie to the daycare facility downstairs, where she can have a great time with the children of her age. My son is there and he will be happy to show Miss Suzie everything that will be of interest for her. I think that will be much better for her than being here alone."

"This is a great idea, Lara. Let's see what Suzie has to say."

"I love to go there, Daddy, and I love to meet Lara's son. Please call me Suzie, Lara. I'm just a child!"

"Why nobody consults my opinion?", Mrs. Jenkins asked.

"Madame does not like suggestions from the servants", Lara said.

"Oh, you go away with your polished English and your French manners. I don't know how long I'll tolerate you and why I still didn't fire you! Paul, give me my drink."

Mr. Jenkins had a short laugh and said:

"I'll meet you downstairs, Patricia. I'm going with them. Come girls, let's go!"

On the way through many halls and corridors and changing elevators, Mr. Jenkins addressed Lara:

"I don't know how you can keep up with my wife. She is not easy to deal with."

"We're getting along just fine, Monsieur. Besides, she only comes to the penthouse once a month. Here is the daycare."

Miss Sarah greeted them with a smile, while Adam rushed to his mother. Later he told her that he became terribly scared when he saw that man next to her and he thought that he was someone from the police who found their refuge and came to arrest them. Lara gave him a long look and she understood in a blink of the eye what was in his mind.

"Something wrong?", he asked.

"No, dear. These are Mr. Jenkins and his daughter Suzie. She will stay here for a while and you'll be kind enough to show her around and make her feel comfortable. Would you?"

"I'm very pleased to meet you, Mr. Jenkins, and you Suzie. Come, I'll show you everything here that you might enjoy."

"I'll stay for a little while with them, if Miss Sarah will allow me. It was a long time since I've been in a daycare. Thank you Lara, you can return to your work."

Back to the penthouse Lara's mind was in turmoil. She thought again how that miserable creature who used to be his father, crushed Adam's childhood, making him to be scared at every step by the authorities who hunted him, threatening his mother with prison and him with being on the streets. At his age, he was supposed to have a happy home and family caring for him, and giving him everything the best a child could have in his life. Instead, he was forced to understand and accept situations that not even grown ups know how to avoid and fight against. She remembered clearely what she told Adam not long ago when he prayed to God to help him in punishing his father: "People do very bad things and sooner or later punishment comes into their lives without us praying for a just retribution be applied to them because of the evil they did". She strongly believed in that prediction, and she hoped to live that day to see it fulfilled. With these thoughts in her mind, she started scrubbing and cleaning behind a capricious and arrogant woman, in her continuous struggle for existence, just to ensure at least the essential sustenance for survival of her child.

In the evening, Lara went to see Adam, according to the usual schedule when Mrs. Jenkins was there. Suzie accompanied him when he rushed to his mother, and told Lara that she had the best time of her life. She made lots of friends and didn't want to go back to the penthouse.

"Can I spend the night here with my friends, Lara?", she asked.

"It is not up to me to decide, Suzie. You have to ask your parents. Your father will be here this evening and then you can talk to him. I'm very glad that you had such a good time."

"Daddy liked very much this place and he said that he wished to spend more time with me and the children.

I think that he will allow me to stay here overnight. Now, I'm going back to play with my friends."

Lara spent a little time with Adam, and then went back to the penthouse. It so happened that Mr. Jenkins was only happy to let Suzie spend the night in the daycare, and make his wife so mad that she started throwing things around and shouting like hell.

She made that scene not because she missed her daughter and wanted her to be close to her, but only because she didn't want Suzie to "associate with children from the low class". Nobody around uttered a single word. As expected, she used Lara as her scapegoat of her madness, cursing, slurring, and throwing at her an entire vocabulary of insults. Mr. Jenkins tried a weak defense in Lara's favor, when his wife shouted:

"You're no better than this ugly creature!"

Lara swallowed her tears and promised herself to pay one day this insane woman for every single word and gesture she used to subject her to most degrading humiliation.

That weekend finally passed, and Lara could enjoy a calm atmosphere at home with her son. She never mentioned to Adam about the hard time she had to endure without being able to fight back.

"How did you like Suzie?"

"She is pretty and nice, but not very smart. She is nine years old and plays with dolls. I wanted to show her some stuff on the computer but she wasn't interested."

"Don't be disappointed if people cannot reach your expectations. Just take them the way they are, and don't try to change them. Everybody has something that can be new for you and you can learn from."

"I know that; you told me this before."

The three weeks until the beginning of school passed quickly. Adam was very excited when he stepped into the classroom for the first time. There were eighteen students, ten girls and eight boys, who came one by one, taking a seat, and arranging their books and pencils on the desk, when their teacher arrived and greeted them.

Mr. Elton Allerton was a young man, brunet, tall, quite well dressed, and smiling most of the time. He told them about the curriculum, mentioning their homework and lots of reading and math. He knew about Adam being the youngest in class of almost seven years old, but didn't ask any questions. He was just curious to see how that little guy will perform in his studies. All the children loved the way that young teacher explained the lessons and how he made everything to look interesting. He gave them homework for the next day, saying that he will test everybody for his and hers level of knowledge. At lunchtime, the students made lots of comments about their first day in class, and tried to get to know each other. In that first day, Adam had his first lesson of German language, and Mr. Albert Fischer showed a lot of patience for those curious children looking at him with eyes wide open. There were only two students beside Adam and they were also beginners. He liked that class too, as he liked everything happening in that day.

When he saw Lara at the door, Adam wanted to tell

her every single detail about his teachers, his classmates, about lessons, and about everything regarding his school. He talked so much covering all the subjects that Lara didn't have to ask anything.

"One thing bothers me", he said. "I'm the smallest in class. All my classmates are taller and have a stronger body; even the girls. Mr. Allerton put me in the first raw, probably to see me better."

"My dearest, in case you forgot, I have to remind you that you are three years younger than your classmates. Is anyone mocking you, or bullying you?"

"Oh, no! Everybody is very nice to me. They call me 'Kid', and I don't mind."

"For the time being we can't do anything about. Maybe later we can find a place where you can go and do workout and gymnastics, and get a bigger body."

Adam mumbled something but accepted his mother's opinion. The next day, Mr. Allerton gave them a math test and a dictation. Adam finished first and his test was graded with A+. When he showed it to his mother, he also said:

"I'll put it in a frame and keep it on the wall for the rest of my life."

After three weeks, Adam's birthday came by, and they celebrated with dinner outside; Lara bought him some books and computer software that he liked a lot. They had a good and smooth life taking care of each other and being happy with the way they managed to establish a harmonious settlement on a more solid basis. Since they came to Boston there were no longer their pictures exposed on TV, and no authority was looking for them. Lara studied a lot the law in parental kidnapping which varies from jurisdiction to jurisdiction. She found out that many states consider parental kidnapping less offensive than classic kidnapping because of the strong bond between parents and children. This was called "abduction" in which an abused parent seeks to safeguard a child from harm, and is different from "kidnapping" which required the use or threat of force. The statute of limitations regarding abduction differs from state to state, but the first few days are crucial for locating an abducted child, and any delay favors the abductor. In most of the cases, after a month or two, the authorities give up in searching for the abducted child, since the chances to find him are extremely low, close to none. All these and many other details made a life a little easier for Lara and Adam, even if they still were scared but not like in the beginning of their desperate situation.

Adam was first in his class, made a lot of friends, and his teacher told Lara that her son had an exceptional intelligence especially gifted for minute details. Lara could not be happier.

Christmas was almost there and the holiday for school was from December 20 till January 6. They had no special plans, but were happy to spend more time together. It was almost one year since they fled from home, and this was a particular occasion for them to celebrate. Adam had to return to the daycare of the hotel while his mother was working, just like before.

Awaiting the coming weekend, Mrs. Dietrich called Lara to her office, asked her to sit down, and said:

"I have to tell you something that might be a shock for you, but this is very confidential and you're not supposed to know before it's time. Mrs. Jenkins wants you to be her private maid at her home on full time basis."

Lara became stunned and barely could manage to articulate some words:

"Mrs. Dietrich, I think I know you well, and I respect you too much as to assume that what you just said is a joke."

"No, Lara, this is not a joke. She wants you to be her maid, she will pay you double of what you make here, you and your son will have a private dwelling, and you both will have food as much as you want. If you ask my opinion, I would say that this is a one-time chance for you and your son, to save a lot of money and later to make a better life for you both. I must add also, that you know her behavior, her bad manners, and her terrible language full of insults, as to be impressed or offended. What do you say?"

"You might be right. I could save a lot of money and Mrs. Jenkins could not offend me more than she already did. I have to talk to Adam first and know his opinion. What will happen to us if she fires me one day when she will be in a worse mood? Then we'll be on the street without job and without a place to live."

"Your place here will be always ready for you, if you have to come back. You have to decide until tomorrow when she will come over, and please don't say a word about our conversation. She told me about this subject last time when she was here, but I waited a little bit to tell you, because I wasn't sure that she will not call me and say that she changed her mind."

Lara told Adam about that new perspective in their life and asked his opinion. He knew very little, close to nothing, about the hard time Mrs. Jenkins gave her.

"It's only up to you, Mom, because I'm not affected in any way, as long as we are together. Actually the perspective of saving the money you pay for food and rent makes me see everything on a very bright side."

Lara was very pleased with Adam's reasoning and she was ready to face the bizarre woman, with her entire patience she had, and hiding her feelings as much as she could. In that Saturday morning, she told Lara that she had a proposal to make, and after describing in detail what she wanted, Mrs. Jenkins didn't even bother to wait for Lara's response.

"I need time to think about", Lara said, "and I have to talk to my son, first."

"Since when your son is your counselor and you have to ask his opinion?"

"Since he was able to think and speak."

"You have time until tomorrow. After that, Aki my chauffeur will help you to move out. Go now!"

She talked as if she was sure that Lara will agree, and that was again one way of throwing an offense at her. Monday afternoon, Aki the chauffeur showed up at the apartment and told Lara about the instructions he had from his employer. He was a very nice man of Japanese origin, short, in his late forties, using a very soft voice, and always smiling when he talked. They decided to move out next day after Lara will resign from her work and will finish packing their belongings. Lara checked out with the manager, even if the rent was paid for the entire month and she didn't ask for any refund. They were ready by Tuesday afternoon, to move to their new home with brighter hopes for a better life. It was a pleasant weather for wintertime without much snow on the streets. Lara had to tie up some loose ends, like Adam's route to his school, and make sure that her working hours will not exceed eight daily. She was determined to make of that new chapter of hers and her son's life a much better one that they had before, no matter what adverse circumstances might come along. Maybe indeed, the good Providence decided to be on their side.

CHAPTER 2

Swinging Steps

Outside the building Aki was waiting for them with a big smile. Lara expected to see a truck, and instead a limousine was there exhibiting elegance and wealth.

"It's Madame's personal car", Aki answered to their amazed look.

He loaded the few belongings they had, showed them the seats behind him, and started the journey. Lara and Adam were indeed amazed by the luxury of that limousine, which had everything to make the best of comfort for the passengers. After about one hour, Aki stopped in front of a big iron forged gate on top of which was written the word "ARTEMIS". Adam asked his mother about the meaning of that word.

"Artemis was the Greek Goddess of the hunt, and she was also known as goddess of wild animals, wilderness, and childbirth."

Aki inserted a card in the security box, the gate opened and he drove along an alee bordered by trees and clusters of shrubs. On both sides and in front they could see a large park with bushes and trees well groomed, just like in a movie, where a team of gardeners raked the garden beds even if they were covered with snow. Aki slowed down the car before a huge mansion Victorian style, unbelievably beautiful.

"This is the main house", he said. "I'll take you to the living quarters of the employees first, where a unit in the building is assigned to you."

He drove to the back of the house, and stopped in front of a two stories small building with four units. On the left side was another small structure, which Aki explained, was the workshop of Mr. Jenkins. In the back of that, a terrace with covered beach chairs and umbrellas surrounded a big swimming pool. Aki helped with their luggage, and showed them their dwelling, which was upstairs on the right corner of the building. It had two rooms of the same size, furnished alike, and all the amenities. Everything was spotless clean.

"I'll let you unpack and get accommodated with your new residence. In the closet, you'll find four uniforms, one for each week. Madame doesn't like her employees to wear the same clothes every day. For this week, take the blue one. When you're ready, call me at this number and I'll come and escort you to meet the whole team."

Both Lara and Adam were very pleased with what they had, especially that there was no rent to pay there. Lara chose the room next to the door in case someone uninvited will come to pay them a visit.

Adam's room was in the corner with two windows

and lot of light coming through. When they were alone, they spoke mostly in French.

"I like very much this apartment", Adam said, "it's smaller than the one we had, but it's cozier and has enough space where I can put my stuff, especially that I have a nice desk here in the corner."

"I like it too, and I'm thinking to buy a laptop for me too. I like making research and learn, mostly because my job is on the opposite side of the human intelligence. I'm thinking also to buy a small, used car for us to go out any time we need, since this place is far from downtown and we cannot ask Aki or anyone else for a drive. Maybe after Christmas we'll go shopping."

The door opened and Suzie showed up running directly into Lara's arms and then embraced Adam. She learned about their arrival and couldn't wait to see them.

"I'm so happy that you came! I hope you'll stay forever here! Adam come, I'll show you around, and we can play outside!"

"We both are very pleased to see you, Suzie but give us a few minutes", Lara said, "we have first to dress properly and then go and meet my co-workers. After that, you and Adam may go and play. Can you wait outside on the balcony for us to be ready?"

"Certainly! I can't wait!"

Lara asked Adam to put his best suit and not forgetting the bowtie. She gave him all the instructions how to behave, how to address every one, and what to talk such as to make a good impression. She put the blue uniform and when they both were ready, she called Aki.

The two of them accompanied by Suzie were escorted to the main house and entered the kitchen through the back door. It was a very big culinary place, equipped with the most modern appliances one can imagine. The tables and counters were covered with lots of all kind of food ready to be prepared for the holidays. There they met the entire personnel who was in the service of the Jenkins' family. They didn't seem to notice Lara's face probably because they have been notified in advance. A tall man in his late forties, good looking, dressed in a black tailcoat directed an introductory speech to the newcomers:

"Welcome to our family, Lara and Adam. My name is Karl Weber and I am the butler. This is my wife Sharon, and she is the cook. You already know Aki Nakamura, and this is his wife Nancy, the cook aide. Everybody, this is Lara the new housekeeper, and her son Adam."

They all shook hands and the newcomers were greeted with smiles and charming words. It took them only few minutes to start liking each others. Sharon was much shorter than her husband, quite corpulent, about the same age as Karl. Nancy was skinny, with red hair, and smiling all the time, just like Aki.

"Lara, this is your bell and light on this row. When you hear the sound and see this light flashing, it means that Madame is calling you, and don't hesitate a moment to rush at her service. Now, would you please come with me, and I'll give you a grand tour of the house", Karl said. "I suggest that Adam and Suzie take a walk to the park and find many attractive aspects there."

Lara and Adam looked at each other with understanding and went each in a different direction.

Karl opened the door to the dining room and told Lara to feel free to ask any questions. She was amazed by the luxury in front of her. The furniture was all sculptured from oak and cherry wood inlaid with silver strings, shell ornaments, and elegantly veneered. A thick Persian rug covered the wood floor from wall to wall leaving only a bare, small space in front of a gas-powered fireplace. Everything was so amazingly luxurious that Lara stood there without moving or saying any work.

Karl awoke her from the state of dreaming and said:

"This house was owned by an English Earl, named John Emerly, who sold it with everything inside including a big library, a music collection, bed linen all new, luxury tableware, and everything that makes the inventory of the kitchen. The Jenkins couple bought it fifteen years ago, and added the most modern appliances in the kitchen, a swimming pool, the workshop, the gym, and the building for the employees. Sharon and I are we them from the beginning. Nancy and Aki came a few months later. Now let's go and see the other rooms."

One by one, all eleven rooms were furnished in the same style, and almost everywhere *Murano* crystals and chandeliers, and *Burano* lace displayed the splendors of an ostentatious wealth. *Limoges* porcelain cobalt blue and gold vases and plates, revealed a great taste and knowledge about that particular art. There were six bathrooms and who knows how many halls and corridors, not mentioning the ornate doors in-between rooms and the stained glass windows, which all had to be cleaned one time or the other. The curved staircase was a pinnacle of artistry with hand forged wrought iron and bronze handrail, showing a delicate ornamental design and a menace for Lara.

After more than one hour touring the house, Karl said:

"Madame is in her study, which is that one, and she is not to be disturbed. You will meet her when she will call you. I leave you now to get familiar with the surroundings. Go to every room, take a good look at everything, and after you have enough, come back to the kitchen. You don't have to do any cleaning today. Tomorrow you'll start doing your job and your work day will be from eight to five with one hour break for lunch."

He left and Lara was alone in one of the bedrooms, talking to herself:

"I need at least one month to learn my way around, and another month to clean this entire house. Maybe she wants me to clean all this living space in one day, everyday. She knew exactly what she wanted, when she picked me and doubled my salary. Only for cleaning the ornaments of the staircase, I need one week. Then either I drop dead, or I still have enough mind left to take Adam and run away from this place as fast as possible."

She took a big sigh, and tried to find her way to the kitchen, wandering through a labyrinth of halls and passageways, until she finally found it. The entire team of servants was there.

"Come Lara", Sharon said, "take a seat and have something to eat. I've already fed the children and they must be somewhere outside playing. It's past lunchtime and you must be hungry. After that, maybe you'll give us a hand here to prepare the food for Christmas. How did you like the house?"

"It's the most beautiful place I've ever seen, but it's not for me. Cleaning the entire place in one day, everyday, is a job for a team of at least four people. I'm not four people, I'm only one, and my strength is limited to a certain line that I cannot trespass. I only can tell you that I proved a lack of common sense, when I lost a good job and a good place of living by accepting this job."

They all surrounded her and Karl said:

"Take it easy, Lara. You don't have to clean everyday the entire place. Most of the rooms are unoccupied and only three bathrooms are used. Go through each one every morning and see which needs cleaning. For the forged iron doors and stairs handrails there is a special spray which works like a self-cleaning. The chandelier in the main hall and the stained glass windows are cleaned twice a year by a special team hired from outside. Listen to my advice and you'll do just fine and even you'll like doing your job. Let me show the supply room which looks like a store and where you can find the most expensive stuff that works like a charm."

Next to the kitchen was the pantry, and next to it was a large supply room with everything one can imagine to ease the hardest cleaning job. Next to that room was a half-bathroom for the employees.

"Thank you, Karl. I feel much better. Tomorrow by the end of my working day, I'll let you know if I can do it or not. Now I'm ready to eat and after that I'll be glad to help you ladies, in the kitchen."

She worked next to her new friends until evening, when the children came in, both laughing, talking loud and showing the best time they had. Karl was ready to serve dinner for the masters, and told Suzie to clean up and show at the table.

"I've already eaten dinner."

"Then go and see your parents, take your shower, and go to bed."

"I'll see you tomorrow Adam. Good night everybody!"

Lara and Adam left after a while and went to their dwelling. In that evening they had a lot to talk about and it was late already when they went to bed. In that evening, before finishing their long talk, Lara took out from her wallet the small picture showing her with Justin in her arms when he was two years old; she kept that picture, hidden with the money in the travel belt around her waist when they left their home. It was the most treasured memory of their past, and she gave it to Adam.

"It's so beautiful! You look like a goddess!", he

shouted, "I would like to have it enlarged and framed, and keep it on my desk."

"We'll do just that when we go to the city next week."

The next morning they went to breakfast, and then Lara started her first day on the job, while Adam went with Aki to visit the gym. She inspected carefully all the rooms and found only four and two bathroom that needed cleaning. In that morning, a few people came in and worked with Mrs. Jenkins in her study, keeping the door closed. Those were accountants, managers, and contractors from the buildings she owned in the city. Later Lara found out that they came two or three times every week and Mrs. Jenkins was one of the most highly regarded businessperson in the city. Following Karl's advice, Lara could do her job without much strain. She took her lunch break and went to the kitchen where Sharon and Nancy prepared a lot of food for Christmas party.

"After my work day, I'll join and help you with everything you'll need", she said.

"We'll need all the help we can get. You see, our workday is from seven to twelve, then we have free time until five and work again until eight, but this week before Christmas, we have to work all day long. Karl and Aki have flexible schedule, and they might help us in the kitchen. We appreciate a lot your offer, Lara. Saturday evening will be a party with about twenty guests coming, and we have to be ready by then with everything."

Lara took her place at the table and followed all the directions given to her by Sharon, for baking a cake, and cutting vegetables in to small pieces. Karl and Aki joined the women and followed the instructions given by both, Sharon and Nancy. In the same time, Lara told them jokes and a story which they enjoyed a lot. It was a warm and pleasant atmosphere shared among people showing friendship and good will.

It was almost dinnertime when the door opened and Mrs. Jenkins showed up. All the servants were there, and also Suzie and Adam.

"I want everything to be perfect, Sharon. A very important couple will be my guests of honor, and I expect the party to be without any reproach. Karl, Aki, and Nancy will serve the guests, while you two will prepare the trays to be ready at the door."

She looked at Lara and said with a mocking tone:

"Make sure that you don't show your face in front of my guests."

It was the first time when they met since she came to her house.

She turned around and left, while everybody looked at Lara who didn't say a word or showed any expression of her feelings. Adam came close to her, took her hand, and said:

"Let's go home, Mom. I have some work to do and I need you to help me."

They left and went to whatever was their home.

"Does she always talk to you like that?"

"Not really. Probably she was in a bad mood after she was in a meeting almost the entire day."

Lara lied and Adam knew that she was lying. Many times, he noticed a mixture of sadness and rage on the face of his mother. He promised to himself that one day he will get wealthy and he will take her out of the reach of Mrs. Jenkins.

The next day, Karl and Aki brought a Christmas tree tall to almost touching the ceiling, and set it in the main hall across the door. In the afternoon they all gathered around and started ornate it. The children had a great time especially that those ornaments had different shapes and colors and they have to be arranged in a certain order according to their size. Even Mr. Jenkins joined them, meeting Lara and Adam for the first time since they came. They all had a great enjoyment, laughing and joking just like Suzie and Adam. Suddenly, Mrs. Jenkins showed up at the top of the stairs, looking at them and not uttering a word. Lara thought that was a good time for her to step on her nerves:

"Perhaps Madame will like to join us?"

"No. I have work to do."

"It is Christmas holiday and perhaps Madame should take a break from work and share a good time with us."

"Oh, you shut up and leave me alone!"

"As Madame desires."

Every one around except the children, who didn't pay any attention, had a hidden smile and appreciated

Lara's comments. It was late evening when they finished decorating the tree. The next day Lara and the other two women worked hard in the kitchen and by seven o'clock, everything was ready for the guests. Before the party, Mrs. Jenkins rang for Lara and asked her to assist her to dress and apply a superficial facial cosmetic. Lara took advantage of that occasion to say:

"With Madame's permission, I would like to take off one working day during the coming week and I will compensate the time on Saturday."

"Why?"

"I have to do some shopping for Adam's school and I would like to buy a small used car to use it whenever I'll need to go to the city."

"You need the car to go around and look for a job?"

"No, Madame. I need it for shopping and going to the bank without appealing to Aki's kindness every time."

"Since you found me in a good disposition, I give you permission to take a day off."

"Madame is very gracious, and I am grateful for Madame's kindness."

"Oh, shut up with your polished English and your French manners! Finish the job, and go!"

Lara was very pleased with the outcome of the conversation and especially with the nervous way Mrs. Jenkins responded. Indeed, Lara had satisfaction every time she could step on that woman's nerves.

The party was a big success and lasted until almost midnight. Everybody slept a little later and when they gathered in the kitchen for Christmas day breakfast, all the bells rang and all the lights flashed. They rushed to the main hall where Mrs. Jenkins was waiting for them next to the Christmas tree. She called first Suzie and Adam, and gave each a bicycle as present. Suzie kissed her and Adam bowed his head and expressed his thanks in very polished English, learned from his mother. After that, Mrs. Jenkins handed to each of her employees an envelope wishing everybody "Merry Christmas".

Each of them received a gift of an entire salary. They all returned to the kitchen for a fabulous breakfast and since it was Sunday and first day of Christmas holiday, everybody had the day off. The masters had to serve themselves if they wanted to eat in that special day. They asked for a story and Lara narrated them Dickens' *Oliver Twist*, much appreciated by everybody. Suzie and Adam went outside trying to enjoy their bicycle but none of them knew how to ride it. Karl and Aki coached them until they could manage to be on their own.

The next morning Aki and Nancy had to drive to the city and took Lara and Adam with them.

"I want you to drop us to a good car dealer, and if I find the car I need, you don't have to drive us back", Lara told Aki.

They found easily a car dealer and Aki didn't want to leave before he was sure that the car Lara chose was in good shape and without damages. Nancy was no less curious. Aki inspected everything on that car and gave his approval. Lara filled in all the papers and they were ready to go. Adam was enthusiastic, he liked the size and the color green of the car, but most of all he liked the tan interior, the radio, and the very comfortable chairs.

Aki and Nancy went shopping while Lara and Adam went to the bank in their little car. She made a deposit in her account and one in Adam's savings.

"Where do you want us to go? We have the entire day to enjoy everything we want", Lara said.

"Let's drive around and enjoy the car, and then we'll go shopping for your laptop and some software for my German learning. Maybe we can enlarge the photo and find a nice frame for it. If you like, we can pay a visit to Miss Sarah and I'll tell her how much I missed her and the daycare. By the way, do you have a license to drive the car?"

"They gave me one from Philadelphia with the other papers in the shelter. Your plan is very good and I would like to see Mrs. Dietrich and have a nice chat with her."

After touring around and finishing shopping they drove to the hotel and each went to see the two people they both liked very much.

Mrs. Dietrich embraced Lara and said:

"Tell me everything and all the details. By the way, since I'm no longer your supervisor, please call me Greta."

Lara told her almost everything, but omitting some embarrassing details.

"I don't understand why she is so hard on you. Is it because your face? Then why did she hire you?"

"On the contrary, Greta. She hired me *because* of

my face. She makes of me the scapegoat of her bitterness every time when her world turns the other way around her, and my face helps her to do just that. She has a very complicated mind where good and bad clash and make her to become unstable."

"I think you managed to know her better than anybody else. She will come this weekend to celebrate the réveillon at the big party in the hotel, and I have assigned a young maid to assist her. I'm prepared for all the consequences."

They chatted about an hour, when it was time for Lara to pick up Adam and drive home.

"Call me anytime you feel like talking", Greta said. I'm very glad that you are comfortable with your work and especially with the other people."

"I will, and you do the same and call me from time to time. Whenever I'll have the occasion, I'll stop by and we can have a nice chat. Bye Greta."

Lara picked up Adam from the daycare where he had a marvelous time with Miss Sarah and the children, and they both went home. It was late evening when they arrived to the house, and the first thing Adam did, was to set the framed picture on his desk. It was beautiful, indeed.

In the coming days, Adam used a lot his bicycle even if the ground outside was covered with a thin layer of snow. The team of servants, who all enjoyed his good nature and his charming approach, adopted him like their nephew. He started calling the two men "Uncle" and the women "Auntie". In very short time, they all became a family, caring for each others. Karl spoke German with him and taught him many new words that Adam managed to pronounce correctly and use them in his vocabulary. Lara couldn't be happier. As usually at lunchtime, Lara told stories that were eagerly awaited by every one in her new family.

One day, Mrs. Jenkins asked Karl:

"How is she doing her job?"

"Excellent. I don't think that she was a maid all her life. She is different from all the others before her. Not only that, but she has a special way of talking, of behaving, of approaching people. She narrates us stories every day at lunchtime, in a cursive language like if she is reading and not speaking. We just don't have enough of listening to her. She never mentioned anything about her past, and we all hold in honor her silence. With all due respect, Madame, I think that she belonged to a higher class much closer to yours than ours. She is an admirable human being and Madame made a very good choice by hiring her and bringing her to the house."

"Thank you Karl for her portrayal you sketched so well. I must go to work now."

She turned around with slow paces and with many thoughts swirling in her mind.

It was Friday evening after dinner, Lara and Adam finished searching and working on their laptops, and were ready to go to sleep, when the phone rang. Lara answered:

"At Madame's service."

"What does she want at this hour?", Adam asked.

"A bubble bath and a massage. Don't wait for me, go to bed, and lock the door. Good night, dearest."

Lara went to the house, directly to Mrs. Jenkins bedroom, and saw her sitting on the edge of the bed. Without any words from either side, Lara prepared her bath with the right scent for the bubbles and said:

"Madame's bath is ready."

She gave her a massage for about more than half hour, helped her out, and put her to bed. In all that time neither uttered a word. When she was ready to leave, Lara heard her saying:

"Tell me a story."

"Madame?"

"You heard me. Tell me a story."

Lara wasn't sure that the tone of her voice was an order or a plea. She took a chair next to the bed and told her the story of the *Little Prince*. It was said that Antoine de Saint-Exupéry cried when he finished writing it. Her voice was soft and warm like a melody of love. She did not know that Mrs. Jenkins recorded the story and listened to her voice three times in that night. Lara did everything she was asked to do, and said before being ready to leave:

"I wish Madame a very good night sleep."

"Tell me one more story."

Lara felt like she was ready to explode.

"With Madame's permission, I must leave, because it is very late and my son is alone and worried."

"Then go!", she shouted so loud that probably her voice could be heard outside.

Lara rushed to the door as fast as she could and ran outside to reach her home before Mrs. Jenkins could call her back. Adam was asleep, she made sure that he was all right and went directly to bed, without analyzing Mrs. Jenkins' bizarre behavior.

First thing in the morning, Adam asked:

"How were the bubble bath and the massage?"

"Lavender scent, but she asked for a bed time story and I told her *The Little Prince.*"

"This woman has not the right number of marbles in her brain."

"What did you say?"

"You heard what I said."

"Where did you learn to speak like that?"

"In school, from my classmates. You see not everybody speaks like you. People use different languages and I have to learn them, because I don't want to become and outsider."

"Come here and sit next to me", Lara said."

"As you desire, Madame."

"I understand your frustration, I have mine too. You can learn all the bad languages you want, but do not use them against people. Trashing people's names and throwing dirt at them will not help. It will only increase your vexation and will lower the confidence in yourself. Since you started to understand and to speak at a very young age, we shared our thoughts and feelings and over the time, we built a strong trust between us. This natural feature is proper to all the creatures existing in the world. Once this feature is broken, it cannot ever be repaired. If you betray it, I'll be never able to trust you again. A few minutes ago, you threw a mockery at me thinking that I deserve it. Think again and you will find out that in my position I have to use the language of a maid addressing her patronne even if I despise it. You put me in the awkward position in which I am not able to tell you anymore what I do, what I think, and what I feel, because I cannot trust you as I always did. Do you understand what I'm saying?"

"Every single word, and I can't tell you enough how much I regret. I promise never to use a bad language against anyone. I also promise not ever to betray the trust you always had in me."

He embraced her with all the warmth of his heart and with heavy tears in his eyes.

It was Saturday morning and after breakfast, Mrs. Jenkins accompanied by Mr. Jenkins and Suzie left for the penthouse. The entire crew had the day off and they all gathered to plan a small party of their own to celebrate the New Year's Eve. In the large kitchen, they all had a tremendous good time, with good food, music, dancing, and many stories, until late night when everybody was tired and they all went to bed. Sunday, the others drove to the city while Lara and Adam stayed home, enjoying talking, reading, and making research on their laptops. Every single day, Lara read online all the newspapers at hand, searching for an ad with their picture that still could mention her status of "abductor" hunted by the authorities. It was already one year since she left home with her child, seeking refuge from the man who had beaten her up with cruelty and disfigured her face. There was no longer any mentioning in any paper of the two fugitives wanted by the police. Lara thought that probably Marc ran out of money to insert new ads or maybe he just gave up searching for them. In any case, she checked every day the papers to make sure that there was no longer any threat for them. She was a fugitive and an abductor before the law, until she will benefit from the statute of limitations, which probably will be after several years.

Monday at noon, the Jenkins family returned home, all of them in a bad mood. Mrs. Jenkins was storming around, while her husband sought shelter in his workshop, and Suzie ran to her room. One day Lara found out from Nancy that in the beginning of their marriage, the couple was very happy. All good time lasted only about one year after Suzie was born, when everything started shaking between them. She became very active all the time with her business, while he kept himself occupied in his wood factory, or in his workshop. Nancy's opinion was that Mr. Jenkins had some frivolous relationships, about which his wife found out but she didn't take any action, except that she decided to have separate bedrooms. A divorce between them was out of the question since they both were bond by the ownership of their business. Over time, they became strangers without any care or loving feelings for each other. Suzie was in the middle but more on the side of her father, even if Mrs. Jenkins was the one who took care of her education and well-being.

In that Monday when they arrived from the penthouse, Lara called her friend Greta:

"What happened? She came in like a storm shouting at every one around and the other two ran to seek refuge somewhere else."

"She fired the poor girl who left in tears, because the girl misplaced her slippers when Mrs. Jenkins needed to go to the bathroom."

Lara burst in to a tremendous laugh while Adam look at her with wonder.

"Don't laugh", Greta said, "I am completely out of resources, and I'm open to any suggestion you can give me."

"Maybe you should try an older woman who has experience and more patience. I'm sorry for what you're going through. Call me anytime you need to ease your frustration. I'm always here for you."

"Thank you, Lara. I'll try to hire an older woman. Bye now."

"What happened? What is so funny?", Adam asked.

"Can I be sure that you'll not get nasty?"

"You have my word."

Lara told him but he didn't laugh.

"I think that she is sick and she needs treatment."

"No, Adam, she is not sick. She wants to control everybody and everything she touches."

The next day was laundry time for Lara who did the laundry for everybody in the house, once a week. Outside was snowing a little but the forecast was a big storm with strong wind and low temperature coming late night. After finishing her working day, Lara went home to do some reading and have a nice chat with Adam like they usually did. She turned the phone off, just to make sure that they will not be disturbed, and by nine o'clock, they went to sleep. A knock at the door, made Lara rise from the bed, she opened the door and Karl came in.

"Why don't you answer the phone? I was trying to reach you several times", Karl said.

"I turned it off because we went to bed and I wanted not to be disturbed. What happened?"

"Madame wants you to come over and give her a bath. I told her that you must be already asleep but she didn't want hear me and asked me to come over and talk……"

Karl didn't finish his phrase, when the door opened and Mrs. Jenkins entered like a hurricane and started shouting like mad:

"Who the hell you think you are by not answering the phone when I called?"

Lara adjusted her voice to medium loud and didn't make any effort to hide her rage:

"And who the hell you think you are by bursting like a wild cat into my home at this hour, and scaring my child?"

Mrs. Jenkins was stunned. She could expect anything coming but not such a vigorous confrontation. In a second, Karl snatched Adam, and both rushed into the other room, closing the door behind.

"I should be there, protecting my mother", Adam said.

"She will be fine, and don't worry. There is a fight between them that will purge all the bitterness they both carried for a long time."

"I'm scared, Uncle Karl. My mom could get hurt."

"Your mom is the bravest person I know and a valiant fighter. She can take a good care of herself. Don't be scared and stop trembling."

Karl noticed the picture on Adam's desk and covered his mouth before making a sound. Adam saw the astounding expression on his face and said:

"My mom with me when I was two years old. Please Uncle Karl don't tell anybody. This picture has a long story that nobody is supposed to know."

"I promise that your secret is safe with me, but I must say that never in my life I've seen such a beauty. It's even above imagination."

Outside the door, it was a war going between two women who confronted each other with big enmity.

"You are supposed to be there for me when I need you, because you are my servant!"

"You are wrong! Yes, I'm your servant, but only for the working day, which is from eight o five, and not one minute before or after! On my time off, you have no right to ask for any service unless I volunteer to fulfill your supplemental demands, which I don't!"

"You are nothing but an insolent, ungrateful, low level creature that only disgusts me!"

"And what makes you think that I consider you

differently than you so delicately labeled me? Listen Madame Jenkins, and listen carefully: I am your servant but you don't own me. You can yell, shout like hell, and throw at me all the trash of your bad language and manners, but I repeat, you don't own me! You can control everybody around you, high-level class, low-level class, and every level class in between, but you cannot control me, and you will never be capable enough to have control over me! My polished English and my French manners, which you so many times mentioned, are my way of addressing you from my place as a maid serving you, and not at all as a proof of consent for your claws to have control over me. Now, step back and go to bed!"

"And you go to hell where you belong! Come Karl, take me home!"

Karl came out of the room, and escorted her outside, while Adam rushed into his mother's arms.

"You are the bravest person in the entire world! You gave her a lesson she'll never forget!"

"We better start packing, my dearest. We're leaving in the morning. Don't ask me where we are going, because I don't know."

They stuffed all their belongings in suitcases, and still could catch a few hours of sleep. In that morning was a terrible snow, just as predicted. They checked everywhere making sure that nothing was left behind, took their luggage, and went to the house. The entire crew was there. Lara opened the suitcases and said:

"We are leaving. Karl and Sharon, please check

thoroughly our luggage, and make sure that we didn't steal anything. I don't want to be chased by the police on the assumption of stealing."

"What on earth did you do, Lara? Where are you going on this storm? You'll not be able to reach even the front gate with this big snow", Sharon said.

No one noticed Mrs. Jenkins who was standing on the threshold of the door and heard everything, until she uttered with a low voice:

"Where you think you're going? You're not leaving anywhere. Nancy, give them breakfast and Karl help them back to their rooms with the luggage."

Lara opened her mouth to confront her, but Sharon made her a sign to keep quiet. After all, she felt tired of fighting that weird woman, she had no place to go with her child, and she could very well handle that creature without any worse aggravations.

Besides, by asking her not to leave, was a step backward for Mrs. Jenkins and one step forward for Lara, which made her feel like a winner.

The following days went by peacefully, making Lara and Adam feeling the surrounding of warmth and concern of their family who cared about them.

One evening, Lara told Adam:

"I have the bad hunch that she will call me one of these days for giving her a bath and a massage and telling her a story."

"What story are you going to tell her?"

"I don't know. Give me a hint."

"I suggest The *Kite Runner* written by Khaled

Hosseini, a sad story set in Afghanistan of the unlikely friendship between a wealthy boy and the son of his father's servant. It will be a very good lesson for her."

"I don't know this story. Where did you read it? We don't have the book in our library."

"I found it online. I narrated it in class at school, and everybody including Mr. Allerton my teacher, liked it a lot. I bookmarked the page to have it anytime at hand. Would you like to read it?"

"Yes, I would like very much to read it. Share with me your intellectual delights."

After finishing it, Lara said:

"I appreciate a lot the topic of the narrative and the style of the author, but I think that this story is a little too mature for your age, don't you think so?"

"I'm not adult and I'm not a grown-up, Mother, but if I understand everything I read, means that the story is not mature for me. If I don't understand everything, it means that the story is indeed mature for me, and I put it on the side for later reading."

Every time he called her "Mother", it meant that he prepared her for an argumentative discussion in which he was ready to defend his point of view.

"You prove to be very selective in your search for acquiring new subjects to enhance your knowledge and I'm very proud of you. But, when you narrated this story you think that your classmates understood the dramatic accent emphasized by the author?"

"I think they did, since they liked it."

"Maybe they liked the very rich action, but maybe

they missed the sensible fluctuations in the souls of the main personages. If you allow me to give you an advice, I'll suggest that in your future narrations in front of the class, stay in the range between Mark Twain's *Huckleberry Finn* and Rudyard Kipling's *The Jungle Book*. I think you understood what I tried to tell you."

"Perfectly. I think you're right. You almost never give me the chance to win in our argumentative discussions, but I like the way you make me understand all the details."

"I love talking with you all the time, but now I have to take care of something I forgot."

Suddenly she remembered that Adam will start school the coming Monday and she had to talk with Karl about switching a little her working schedule, since she had to drive Adam to school and back home.

"Everything is taken care of", Karl said, "Adam's school is almost across Suzie's school and they have the same schedule. Aki will drive them both and you don't have to worry about anything."

"Adam has German lessons twice a week and these are after the school regular time."

"Suzie has piano lessons by the same time and as you can see, there is nothing for you to worry about. Don't ask me how I know all about this, or how I got all the instructions, because everything is routine and nothing is exciting."

"Thanks Karl, I don't bother to ask for details, because I can guess their source."

The next day, it was reported in the news that an

even bigger storm is expected. Late in the evening, the phone rang and Lara was called for the bubble bath, the massage, and the bedtime story.

"At your service, Madame", she answered.

The house was empty and dark, since it was close to bedtime and everybody was home and ready to sleep. Lara went directly to Mrs. Jenkins' bedroom, helped her with the bath, gave her a good massage, and put her to bed. In all that time, neither uttered a word other than referenced to the job.

"Now tell me the story."

Lara took a chair close to the bed and started narrating *The Kite Runner* for more than a half hour. Mrs. Jenkins kept her eyes closed but she followed Lara's every word through her eyelids. The small recorder hidden somewhere close, registered every sound of the voice which was like a melody of love. It took Lara a longer time than Adam needed to narrate the entire story, because she made many pauses, hoping that Mrs. Jenkins was asleep and she could go. When she finished, she turned off the light and with silent steps, she went out. After Lara left, Mrs. Jenkins turned on the recorder and listened to her voice for more than an hour, and only after, she fell asleep.

Lara checked on Adam first, and then she went to sleep, without moving the entire night. In the morning, the crew was outside already, shoveling the snow and clearing the road to the gate. Lara and Adam dressed quickly and joined them. Suzie saw them and came down to give them a hand. Nobody had breakfast yet but the work had to be done before the level of snow rose. From time to time, they threw the shovels on the side and started playing with snowballs, chasing each other, laughing a lot, and having a marvelous time.

Mrs. Jenkins was at the window, looking at them and not moving at all. Lara spotted her, gave her a long look, and showed her the malicious smile she didn't hide when she wanted it to be noticed. The others saw her also, and were curious for a minute about what she might think when looking at them for such a long time and stood there without moving from the window. They shrugged and continued shoveling. Only Lara understood better than anyone else did, that complicated mind where *good and bad clash and make that woman to become unstable.* She stood like a stone in front of that window, alone in a ghostly house, without anyone close to her, to care for her, and to answer to the love she was eager to give. She had everything a wealthy woman can have, and she was ready to give her wealth, her luxurious house, and even her bad behavior, in exchange for one single drop of love. She stared at those people who had a great time, who were poor compared to her, but had a lot of happiness in their life because they care for each others and they loved each others. In that moment, she would have given anything just to be like them. Lara looked at her and gave her again that malicious smile that she didn't bother to hide.

It was already lunchtime when they all, wet, joyful, and hungry, returned to the house. The news said that the entire city was covered with snow, government agencies and businesses were closed, buses and cars were stalked on the roads, and even pedestrians had a very hard time to stand up against the winds. All schools will be closed for the next days, until a next communicate will state otherwise. In the coming week, the storm diminished, the city returned to its normal sate, and the school started three days late. One day, Adam came home with bruises and scratches over his body. Lara was full of anger and ready to explode.

"Tell me all about and who did this to you, and especially why."

"My classmate Jack Lipmann started mocking everybody who was not rich like his parents. He called me names and mocked me because my mother was a maid, and he mimicked derisively with gestures that imitated what my mother was doing. I got mad and punched him in his stomach, and then he started punching and scratching me and shouting until the teacher who was outside came in and took us apart."

Lara checked on Adam, found that he was all right and the next day she went with him to school, without asking any permission from Mrs. Jenkins. Karl told her later what happened and she said:

"I'm going to teach the Principal a good lesson!"

"I suggest Madame not to intervene. Lara is a vigorous warrior and she knows what to do."

Lara entered the Principal office and showed him what happened to her son.

"I would like to speak with the boy who did this to Adam."

"I'm very sorry Mrs. Collins for what happened, and I promise to take action", he said.

"I would like to speak to him, if you don't mind."

The Principal made a call and a tall, strong boy showed up, looking with apathy at the people in the room. Lara started her speech:

"My name is Lara Collins and I am Adam's mother. I presume your name is Jack Lipmann, you are Adam's classmate, and you had a discontent regarding my occupation as a maid. I would very much appreciate your explanation."

"I have nothing to explain to you. It is in my family to treat with regard only people of our league."

"Is your mother working?"

"Yes, she is an accountant with a big firm."

"And your father?"

"My parents are divorced and I live with my mother."

"You see Jack, I'm working too, even if I do a different job than your mother, and I belong to a different league than your family. Your mother works hard to provide you with food, clothing, and shelter, and especially with a good education, so that you can grow up in a safe surrounding without missing anything that might be part of a good life. So am I. You see, I'm doing exactly for Adam that your mother is doing for you, only on a different platform. We both care, love, and provide support for our children with the same high hopes and wishes to see them growing up. In this regard, there is no difference between your mother and me. If only for this reason alone, we both deserve the same regard and consideration, because we both stand for the same principles that we respect and praise with dignity and self-esteem. Adam didn't do anything wrong. He only defended the honor of his mother who was not there to defend herself. I'm convinced that you have acted in the same way to defend the honor of your mother. This is all I had to say to you. I wish you the best in life and may you never be disappointed by your own behavior."

Lara stood up and addressed the Principal who showed astonishment on his face:

"Mr. Burton, thank you for your time and for giving me the opportunity to meet Jack and explaining him some details about my job that probably were greatly misunderstood by him."

Then she said to Adam:

"Come Adam, let's go home. With the permission of your Principal, you will miss the class today."

"One moment please, Mrs. Collins", Jack said, "I apologize for behaving like a jerk. I wish having the same grade of pride for my mother as Adam has for you. Thank you for explaining to me so clearly a subject that was very confused and nobody ever cared to make it understandable for me. Please forgive me if you can, and Adam you too, maybe you can forgive me."

"You have my entire forgiveness, Jack. You are a bright and good young man with a sensitive mind. I commend you for the courage you proved by sincerely recognizing your misjudgment. I'm glad I've met you, even under unfortunate circumstances", Lara said.

Adam approached him and they shook hands.

"I forgive you too, Jack. Maybe one day we can be friends."

Jack left and the Principal said:

"I learned a very useful lesson from you, Mrs. Collins. You should be a teacher. Adam can go home for today, and I expect him in school tomorrow."

On their way out, Adam said:

"You gave him a lesson he will remember for a long time. Maybe he will ad it to his collection that makes the package of his education. I'm immensely proud of you, Mom."

"It's almost lunchtime and let's go some place and have a good meal. After that, we go and do shopping. I need to buy some books to catch up with my reading, and you think about something nice that you want."

They had lunch, and then they went to a bookstore where Lara bought a few Philosophy books that she could no longer endure to miss. Adam couldn't make up his mind for what he wanted, so that she chose for him an ingenious electronic gadget, elaborately designed for hundreds of mind games that were educational and entertaining in the same time.

"I never knew that something so interesting might be on the market. It's just awesome! I can play and I can learn a lot! Thank you my dearest, Mom. May I take a look at the books you bought?"

He looked at the titles and perused the inside of René Descartes' *"Meditation on First Philosophy",* and Immanuel Kant's *"Critique of Pure Reason".* He didn't bother to look at the others; they just seemed to be alike.

"Now, these I can call 'mature' stories, because I don't understand a single word!"

"I'm glad we finally agree about the definition of a 'mature' story. These will be your favorite books also, when you'll grow up and understand them. Then, you'll absorb every word with all the pores of your well-trained mind. I would like you not to make any mentioning about these books to anybody at the house. Now, let's go home."

They arrived late afternoon and everybody was anxious to find out how Lara solved that incident.

She told them everything and they all surrounded her and gave her a big hug. Aki said to Adam:

"I'm going to teach you Karate and how to defend yourself. You'll become strong and self-confident and nobody will dare to harm you."

"Would you do this for me, Uncle Aki? I'm eager to learn and I promise to be a good pupil."

"We'll start this weekend and we'll practice half hour every day."

Adam jumped into his arms, embraced him until Aki showed a big emotion, and pushed him toward his mother.

"Are you excited, Mom?"

"It's enough for me that you are. This is one type of excitement that I can skip easily. Let's go home, I'll put my uniform and go to work, and you do whatever you feel like doing."

Mrs. Jenkins couldn't resist her curiosity and asked

Karl about the incident at Adam's school. He told her everything and said:

"She is a good fighter, especially when she uses soft words. I've never known someone like her. She is a mystery to me but a wonderful one."

"What's new?", Mrs. Jenkins mumbled.

In that evening, Lara caressed her beloved books and arranged them in a special section on the shelf.

Adam started his first Karate lesson in the coming weekend, to become a warrior *in defending fairness and justice*. Lara decided to watch him later, when he will know the basics of the program. Adam had lessons from Aki not only how to defend himself, but also he learned how to speak Japanese.

In the following weekend, Mrs. Jenkins made her trip to the penthouse, and Lara spent a good and rewarding time reading from the books of the Masters. Adam played mind games on his gadget exploring and testing subjects in cognitive science that he liked the most. Lara suddenly remembered that Suzie was alone in the house, since it was already Sunday and probably everybody went to the city. It was Nancy's shift for that weekend, but certainly, she had better things to do than looking after Suzie.

"I would like to call Suzie to come over, and maybe you can show her some of the marvels on your gadget."

"She is a bore, and I'm not her baby sitter. Besides, she wouldn't understand any of these", was Adam's response.

"Don't you have any consideration and kindness?"

"Not today, Mother. Maybe tomorrow I'll have some."

"I won't argue with you, since you're so busy. I'm going to check on her. Please answer the phone, that is, if you have time and can hear it."

Lara went to the house directly to Suzie's room and she found her sitting on the edge of the bed holding a doll.

"How are you today Suzie? You seem very pensive and having lots of heavy thoughts on your mind."

"I'm so glad you came, Lara. I feel lonely and find nothing pleasant to do. I'm always alone, my mother is always busy, she doesn't know that I even exist, and my father is never home."

"Let's see maybe we can find something together. How about you play a nice piece for me on the piano?"

"I hate piano and the lessons at school, and especially my teacher. For months already she gives me only boring lessons and exercising Czerny."

"Well then, would you like me to play something for you?"

"Can you play piano? I would like very much to listen to a beautiful piece for a change. Come, let's go to the living room."

"Do you have a special musical piece that you like listening?"

"Anything, but Czerny."

Lara played for her Chopin's *Grand Valse Brillante*. She didn't play in a long time, and she thought that her hands were rusty and her fingers lost their touch, but at her amazement, she played beautifully. Suzie was astounded, like filled with wonder.

"You play like a pro! Why are you working as a maid for my mother when you can play like that?"

"It's a long story, Suzie. Besides, with my look, I couldn't face any size of an auditorium."

"To me, you are the most beautiful person I know. Please, Lara play again something."

She played Schubert's *Moment Musical*. Suzie closed her eyes, and let herself lost in a reverie. Lara forgot where she was and played again without being asked, one piece after another. None of them noticed that Mrs. Jenkins was standing at the door like a stone, watching them both and listening to Chopin's *Polonaise Heroique* that Lara was playing. When she finished, Suzie was the first to see her mother:

"When did you come? I thought you will stay at the penthouse until tomorrow as usually. Lara played for me like a pro, the most beautiful piano music I've ever heard."

Mrs. Jenkins gave her a long look and said:

"So, she can play piano too. What else should I know?"

"I have to go now. Suzie, it was a great pleasure that we both shared. Try practicing the music you love."

"Don't go. Play something for me", Mrs. Jenkins said.

"Anything special?"

"Just play!"

Lara played for her Schubert's *Serenade,* and was ready to go when she said:

"Play again!"

Lara played Chopin's *Tristesse,* a piece that no one could resist the melancholy of its harmonious melody. When she finished, Mrs. Jenkins was still sitting in the armchair with closed eyes. Was an illusion what Lara noticed? She spotted tears at the corner of her eyes! That woman with a soul made of steel, actually could cry when beauty overwhelmed her emotions and made her fall in to a reverie only touched by her melted feelings.

With slow movements and silent steps, Lara went out with many questions and without answers in her mind. Adam looked at her with curiosity, waiting to hear the whole story which he didn't expect to be so exciting.

"Mrs. Dietrich called and she wants to talk to you."

Lara called her and found out that Mrs. Jenkins left earlier, because the old maid who "was slow, mumbled, and mixed up the colors of the bed sheets" infuriated her.

"I don't think that was the reason for her leaving earlier, Greta."

"Then why?"

"Maybe she is looking for something new, to invigorate her, and got bored of what she has. I have no idea what is she expecting, but I think I'm right."

"What if she will ask you to come with her next time?"

"I'll come with her, Greta."

"Don't you have enough of her everyday all day long out there?"

"I want her to like the trips to penthouse just as before, and not looking for something new to fulfill her pleasures. My life here is quite peaceful and I don't want it to be disturbed by some fancy delights that she might want, and which will give me a hard time by running after her and keeping up with her."

"You know what you're talking about and I'm not even curious to find out. Bye Lara, talk to you soon."

Lara spent what was left of that Sunday, reading from the Masters and taking notes, while Adam used his gadget to test his mind.

When the time for Mrs. Jenkins' next trip to the penthouse was close, Lara told her family that she will go with her. It was Friday evening and they all had dinner together as usually.

"I'll miss school and I don't like that", Adam said.

"What do you want me to do? Leaving you home alone? You know I can't do that", Lara said.

"I'll tell you what", Sharon intervened, "this weekend is my turn to work and stay home. I'll be happy if Adam will like staying with us, instead of going with you and stay in daycare. We have plenty of room to accommodate him and I know that he'll find something to keep him busy. Monday morning he can go to school as usually and not miss his class. What do you say?"

Before Lara could answer, Adam jumped:

"I would love staying home with Auntie Sharon and Uncle Karl, Mom. May I?"

"You just made my life easier, Sharon, but are you sure that this will be not an inconvenience for you and Karl?"

"Not a bit. It will be a great pleasure to have Adam with us. Suzie can stay too, but she has to ask her mother first. We have plenty of room for both."

They finished dinner when Suzie showed up looking for Lara.

"Mommy said that we'll have to leave one hour earlier tomorrow for the penthouse because she has to attend some business first."

Lara told her about the option she had to stay home like Adam, with Sharon and Karl, but she had to ask her mother. Suzie was thrilled.

"I'll be more than happy, and I'm sure this will make my mother happy too!"

In that evening, Lara packed in a small suitcase a few belongings of her own. She planned to change a little bit the regular schedule of her sojourn in the penthouse.

Next morning, Lara was already in the limo sitting in the front, when Mrs. Jenkins showed up.

"Where are the children?"

"They will stay home with Sharon and Karl, because they didn't want to miss school."

"Whose decision was that? Nobody asked me."

"It was their decision, Madame."

It was obvious that Suzie didn't bother to ask permission from her mother.

"Go, Aki! It's useless to hear the details of this story!"

There was no other conversation during the entire trip. Seemingly, Mrs. Jenkins was in a tempestuous mood. Her husband didn't come home for already three nights!

At the hotel entrance, Paul was waiting. After greeting Mrs. Jenkins with the usual welcoming salutation, he shook hands with Aki, and addressed Lara:

"*Je suis très content de te voir, Lara.*"

"*Je suis content de te voir aussi, Paul.*"

"Don't tell me that you speak French!", Mrs. Jenkins exploded, "Do you?"

"Madame just said not to tell Madame that I speak French, and so I'm not telling Madame that I speak French."

"Paul! Tell this creature in whatever language she speaks, that she just stepped on my nerves in the first minute I got here!"

"I'll tell her, Madame, but first we have to move on because we are blocking the entrance."

Paul smiled at Lara, she smiled back, and both gave an amusing look to Aki.

Paul took Mrs. Jenkins' luggage and followed her to the private elevator that went straight to the penthouse.

"Give me my drink, Paul, and wait for me to take

me downstairs. We'll go first to the General Manager's office and then after, to the Casino at my usual place."

They left, and Lara started unpacking, asking herself why Mrs. Jenkins was so eager to visit the General Manager. She found later from Paul, that Madame was very displeased with the low profit of the Casino in that month, and she blamed the poor guy for not having the proper approach to the wealthy patrons.

Around three o'clock Mrs. Jenkins came upstairs, took her nap and by five she left for her bridge party.

Lara called Adam who said that he has a very good time:

"Uncle Karl taught me to play chess and Auntie Sharon showed Suzie how to make dresses for her dolls. I miss you, Mom, but I'm better here than in daycare. Tell me about you."

"Boring. I'm glad you have a good time. I brought a book with me and I'm going to do some reading, and pay a visit to Greta. I'll call you tomorrow. Bye, dearest."

Around eight that evening, Lara dressed nicely, covered her face with a piece of fine voile, wore a pair of white gloves long to the elbows, put a coquette white beret on her head, and went downstairs to the Casino. She made a grand tour, just being curious to see how poor and rich people mixed in that huge place by losing their money. The poor lost pennies trying their luck at slot machines, while the wealthy lost fortunes at the gambling tables. Lara went to the room where people had drinks and snacks while a small orchestra played soft music inviting couples to dance. A man in his forties, tall and good looking, approached her and said:

"Would you give me the honor to dance with you?"

"With pleasure", Lara answered.

"I would like very much to see your face. I think you're very beautiful."

"Maybe later."

They went to the floor dance and followed the music with small steps of a tango.

"You are a superb dancer", the man said.

"So are you."

Lara remembered how Marc used to hold her tightly when they danced. He used to whisper how beautiful she was and how much he loved her. They both were marvelous dancers, gliding on the floor and barely touching it. His image came like a shadow before her eyes, reminding her happiness they both believed that will last forever. Their life was like a heavenly landscaped garden where they walked hand in hand, being sure that nothing will ever come between them to take them apart. One day came when their life was torn to pieces, and they walked away from each other, farther and farther until they both disappeared. She kept dancing with that stranger until she realized that she couldn't stand him and the way he hold her. She just wanted to get rid of him when he asked:

"Would you like to have a drink with me at the bar?"

"Certainly", she said, "but give me a moment first to powder my nose, and I'll be back."

She left him at the bar, and rushed to the elevator,

which took her to the penthouse. It was almost time for Mrs. Jenkins' return. Lara put her uniform and went to the room waiting for her. She looked like she had one drink too much. Lara helped her dress for the night and put her to bed.

"Tell me a story."

"It's very late and I'm very tired."

"Why are you tired? You didn't do anything to be tired."

"I danced all night."

"You what?"

"I danced. Go to sleep now."

Lara left her and went to the supply room to catch some sleep for the rest of the night.

In the morning Mrs. Jenkins woke up around ten, and she looked fresh and in good mood.

"You said last night that you were dancing?"

"I didn't say that. Probably Madame had a bad dream."

"Very strange. I'm almost sure that I heard you saying that you danced all night."

"I was sleeping Madame, and not dancing. Madame had a bad dream as I said with certainty."

"Maybe you're right. Help me dress and call Paul to give me my drink."

She left to play her usual roulette and Lara went to see Greta. They embraced each other and had lunch and a long talk like between good friends.

"This is the last time I came with her, Greta. Try to find someone who can handle her. I'm thinking maybe you can find someone who desperately needs a job and will accept a difficult character like she is, no matter how hard serving her it would be."

"I know a middle age woman who is alone, has no family and just lost her job, but she never worked as a maid. She was a clerk before, and I doubt that she will be able to do this job, much less that she will be able to handle that capricious woman."

"It's worth trying. Talk to her and tell her everything she might expect, without hiding the bad side of the matter. Maybe she will accept to do the job, especially that it will be only once a month."

"I'll try talking to her, Lara, but don't be surprised if she will be fired like all the others."

"Let me know, and call me at any time. It was a real pleasure having this nice chat with you. I must be going now."

Lara left, thinking that it will be very hard for that woman to handle Mrs. Jenkins' bad behavior unless she wanted to keep that lousy job that paid very little, and she had no other choice.

The weekend was over and they returned home. Adam jumped into his mother arms, telling her what a good time he had, especially that he learned how to play chess and now he could play with the computer.

"Do I detect a slight foreign accent in your speech?", Lara asked.

"I try to improve it. I thought that because I live in this part of the country where most of the people speak with British accent, I should have it also. I like it very much, and it sounds very worldly-wise. Don't you think so?"

"Let's make it clear from the beginning. Boston doesn't have one accent. It has several accents. Boston is an old city, and had numerous waves of immigrants. Each brought their own accent, and they lived (and still live) in semi-segregated communities. The Boston accent is the result of mixing accents from New England, Irish-Americans, and Midwesterners. The New England accent, especially around Boston, is closer to the modern British accent. Some of this is probably due to a greater numbers of immigrants from the British Isles settling in and around Boston. The British accent is different. It more closely resembles the sounds of the South East of England where many of the schools and universities are based. Over the time, the accent itself became a marker of class and power and it was called "Received Pronunciation". It is the accent of Standard English in the United Kingdom and is the accent of English as spoken in the south of England. Take a look at your world globe and see all these area that I mentioned."

"Can you speak with British accent?"

"I can my dearest, and I like it very much. Remember that once I was teaching English Literature, and for that reason, I had to learn how to speak with British accent. I don't use it around, because as you said, it sounds very worldly-wise. Give me a book and I'll give you a demonstration."

She read a full page, and Adam exploded of excitement:

"It's beautiful Mom! I wish I could speak like you! Will you train me?"

"I'll be happy to, and we can practice but only when we are alone. Make sure that you don't confuse it with the Boston accent. You can learn both, but make always a distinction between them."

In the coming weekend, it was cold outside with signs of a freezing day. Lara went to check on her car and to put the cover on it, but she didn't wear any coat to protect her and she got a bitter cold in that morning. A small cough and runny nose put her to bed for the rest of the day. Next morning she felt worse, and couldn't go to the house for the breakfast. Karl came over to check on her and she barely could speak. It was Saturday and Adam was home, worried and scared when he looked at her and not knowing what to do. Karl called his wife who gave her a light home treatment and a sleeping pill to make her rest.

Sharon told Adam not to worry about because his mother had just a simple cold, and she will come later to check on her. In the meantime, Mrs. Jenkins went to the kitchen, found out from Sharon that Lara was sick, and had to stay in bed.

"Karl, take me to her", she said.

"Madame, she is resting because she didn't sleep last night and I think it's not a good time to visit her."

"I didn't ask what you think. I asked you to take me to her."

Adam opened the door and let them inside.

"Where is your mother?", she asked.

"In her bed, sleeping and coughing from time to time."

Mrs. Jenkins came close to Lara, looked at her pale face, and told Karl:

"Call doctor Maurs to come right away, and tell Aki to take the limo and bring him over."

"I don't know, Madame if he will come on such a short notice, especially on weekend."

"Then make it even shorter, and just don't stand there and wait for the next weather!"

Karl shrugged and left. Mrs. Jenkins looked around, and read the titles of the books on the shelf, touching them one by one.

"These are her books, Madame", Adam said, "she calls them 'The Masters', and she reads them all the time and takes many notes. She said that they are written by the most intelligent minds that ever existed."

On Lara's desk was Nietzsche's *Perspectivism* work, where he claimed that the death of God would eventually lead to the loss of any universal perspective on things. A few papers on the side were notes extracted by Lara from the book.

"Do you read them too?"

"Oh, no Madame. Those are mature stories and I'm too young for understanding them. When I'll grow up I'll be mature and then I'll read them, and *I'll absorb every word with all the pores of my well trained mind.* (He just repeated Lara's words!). My mom is very mature, Madame, and she understands everything."

"You don't say. Why am I not surprised?"

"Will you excuse me, please? I have to make tea for her, to have it ready when she wakes up."

Adam went to their small kitchen and came back with a plate of cookies.

"Auntie Sharon baked them this morning especially for my mom. Please have some, they are very good."

Lara was awake but didn't move. She heard part of the conversation between Mrs. Jenkins and Adam and she was just curious to hear the follow-up story.

"Who made you, Adam?", Mrs. Jenkins asked.

Lara opened her eyes and said:

"I made him."

"You woke up, Mom! I'm going to bring you the tea!"

He rushed to the kitchen and Lara took advantage to show her anger to that woman who kept staring at her as if she saw her for the first time:

"What are you doing here and who invited you? I don't have enough strength to fight you today. *Maybe tomorrow I'll have some.*"(She used Adam's words!)

"Karl said that you were sick and I came to see if he was not exaggerating."

"And what is your prognosis? Did Karl lie, or did he tell you the truth?"

"Doctor Maurs will be here in minutes and he will tell the prognosis for us both."

"I don't need your doctor. Just go and leave me alone."

"Since when do you speak with British accent?"

"Since always I liked speaking with British accent. Does it bother you?"

"In a way, yes."

Lara knew exactly that the "way" she was bothered with this time, was the same as all the others that were hard attempts to reach her soul, and they all failed.

Adam brought a tray with the tea, showing the care he had for his mother:

"Here is your tea, just the way you like it. Tell me if it's hot enough."

"It's perfect, my dearest. Thank you."

A knock on the door interrupted their conversation. Adam opened the door and Doctor Maurs came in, followed by Karl. He was in his fifties probably, had white hair, quick movements, and a friendly voice.

"Where is the patient? Oh, Patricia is so nice seeing you! You look lovely!", he said with a jolly tone.

Adam showed him where the patient was, and came close to Karl, taking his hand. Doctor Maurs invited everybody to get outside the room and checked thoroughly Lara's body. After he finished, he opened the door, and let them all inside.

"It's just a minor cold, nothing serious, but she needs lot of nutrition, vitamins, and rest. It seems to me that she didn't have a check up in a long time. I'll write a prescription for cough and something to give her more strength. Aki can take it from the pharmacy on his way back after he drives me home."

Adam approached him and said:

"Sir Doctor, I'll take good care of her and make sure that she follows your orders."

"Who might be you, young man?", the doctor asked.

"My name is Adam Collins, and I am the son of Lara Collins who is your patient."

Doctor Maurs stared at that boy who looked like a watercolor portrait and said:

"Well, Sir Adam Collins, I entrust you with the care of your mother, and I can assure you that if she follows my orders, she will recover in no time."

"I promise to make her follow your orders, Sir Doctor."

"Thank you Doctor Maurs, for your kindness and your help", Lara said. "Please send me the bill for the consultation."

"I'll take care of the bill, Richard. Just send it to me", Mrs. Jenkins said.

"My dear Patricia, you never paid my bills, since I know you, that is what I remember in twenty years."

"Because you never sent me a bill."

"Don't bother; I'm not going to charge her."

They all left. Lara and Adam finally were alone.

Karl escorted Mrs. Jenkins to the house and was ready to leave when she said:

"Who is she, Karl? She knows hundreds of stories that she narrates at the most academic language; she plays piano like a pro; she speaks French fluently; she reads Philosophy; she knows English with British accent; she raises her son to become a prince of intellect; and she works as a maid in my house doing an excellent job, tolerating all my frustrations and bad moods, without ever complaining when she is wearing her uniform. Who is she, Karl?"

"She is a woman with deep scars on her face and even deeper scars on her soul, Madame."

Time passed by, the month of April came with Lara's birthday according to the new certificate that she received in the shelter.

"Happy Birthday, my dearest Mom. How old are you now?"

"Thank you my dearest son. I'll be thirty years old next month, and I count my age according to my real certificate and not to the one given to me afterwards."

"How would you like to celebrate your special day, even if it's not the real one?"

"Just staying home with you and doing what we do every day, and nothing special. Nobody knows about my birthday and I like to be like that."

After two months, Adam graduated first in his class and entered the fourth grade. Summer vacation was there and Lara had two weeks paid, but no special plans other than staying home. They had no place to go and enjoy a free time, and they both decided that it was better to save money and stay home where they had everything they needed. Lara had to start cooking, since she didn't want to take any advantage of the free three meals they had, while she was not working. Most of the time she liked studying and making notes. Adam had his own plans for his vacation:

"I want to make my body taller and stronger. I'll use

a lot the gym and the pool, and Uncle Aki will teach me the next level of the Karate training. By the way, Mom, I can speak a little simple Japanese that Uncle Aki taught me. I intend to learn more and speak better, until I'll speak very well."

"You amaze me", Lara said. "I wish I could learn Japanese too, but I don't have time for that. I'm happy that you can learn and that you like it. Your plan to build your body sounds very good to me. I intend to take a little care of my body too, by using the gym and swimming. Before anything, I will like us to have a thorough check-up by a doctor for you and one for me."

She picked from the phone book two doctors who worked at the hospital and made an appointment for the next day. They both came out with an excellent bill of health, with only the mention that both needed vitamins and a supplement of calcium.

"Now we can work on our bodies and make them stronger, with all the confidence that we are both healthy", Lara said.

In that evening, she tried to find some music on the computer, but the selection as from a particular performer, orchestra, or type of arrangement was not as wide as expected, and the sound was poor and limited to the audio system which had no amplifiers.

"Let's go tomorrow and buy a media player, and some discs with beautiful music that we can enjoy."

The next day, they went to the store and took their time to look around until they found what they wanted. Regarding music, each one had preferences and both agreed about Classic, Opera, and some Country Music. They bought mostly videos that they also could watch, and not only listen.

Back home, Lara made all the installations for the system, and for the first try, Adam chose Chopin *Piano Concerto 1-played by Martha Argerich.* It was a real treat for them especially that both loved music and they couldn't have any in a long time.

"It's awesome, Mom! She plays like an angel! I missed my piano practice and when I see this marvel I would like to have it back!"

"It's indeed a marvel, Adam. I'm so glad we can have music again in our home! I wish to give you back the pleasure of playing piano, but how? We cannot have a piano here, and I don't see where you can practice and learn."

"I know that in school there are teachers, who give lessons for piano and violin for students, but I think these classes have to be paid and I don't want you to spend money for these, when you work so hard and we have to save everything."

"You'll have your piano lessons when the new school year begins! Don't worry about money, because we have plenty. I saved a lot since I've been working here, and we had a substantial amount from before. Your account is coming good also, because every time I get my paycheck I deposit a little bit of money in to your savings. When you'll be eighteen, you'll have a lot of money. When we'll leave this place, we can have a beautiful home somewhere else and you can go to an expensive university without any care for tuition."

Adam jumped into her arms, kissing her both cheeks and caressing her hair.

"There is nowhere in the entire world a mother like you!"

"I know."

Every single evening after dinner, they watched a concert or an opera, lowering the sound so as not to disturb the people downstairs.

Lara kept herself busy in the morning by cooking and cleaning their home, while Adam took care of his sporting interests only when an adult was around. Sometimes, Lara joined him in the gym or in swimming. She didn't know that Mrs. Jenkins watched them at the window, every time they were in the area of her visibility.

"How are they?", she asked Karl.

"They are on vacation and they are doing great. We can hear a very faint sound of music every evening coming from upstairs that Sharon and I enjoy a lot. We wish they put it louder, but we don't want to intrude."

"She made us all feel like outsiders, Karl."

"No, Madame. When she first came, all she wanted was to be treated the same as we were. We received her in our families like one of our own, and shortly after, she and her son became members of the entire family as we are. With all due respect, you made her feel like a stranger and like an outsider. Now, it's her turn."

"Are they coming for their meals?"

"No, Madame. She said that when she is on vacation and not working, she cooks and doesn't take advantage of what she doesn't earn."

"Why this woman has always something fresh to give me headaches and being a pain in my neck? Why can't she be like everybody else?"

"Because she is not only very different from everybody else but she is distinctive in an intriguing way, hard to be deciphered. I've never known someone like her."

"I wish I never brought her here, Karl."

"It's too late Madame."

"You preached me a lecture that I've already known."

Lara's vacation ended and she had to go back to her work. The coming weekend was time for Mrs. Jenkins' trip to the penthouse, and Karl told Lara to be ready to accompany her.

"I'm not going, Karl. I want to stay home with Adam and have both a good time. You see, when I go to the penthouse I get very tired, and I have a hard time keeping up with her going downstairs and coming upstairs at hours when I need rest and sleep. Tell her that I'm not going this time or any other time."

"She won't like that."

"I know Karl, I know."

Lara expected a storm with the usual rudeness and shouting, and she was ready to put up a big fight, but nothing happened.

In that summer, Mrs. Jenkins decided to have a

bridge party every week on Thursday. Her husband was an active member of her club and he became a professional in that game by winning several local championships. He came to Mrs. Jenkins parties, not so much for playing but mostly for seeing his daughter and for spending some time with her. In that particular Thursday, Mrs. Jenkins was his partner sitting opposite each other, when suddenly he said with a mocking tone:

"Patricia, you should consider playing Rummy instead of bridge. You'll never learn how to play this game. In fifteen years you didn't improve a bit."

"Maybe you should give me some lessons."

"I would love to but I'm always very busy running back and forth between customers who pay big for my products."

"Or rather you're busy running back and forth between your mistresses?"

He threw his cards on the table and shouted:

"I have enough of you! I'm leaving!"

He stood up and on his way out, he shouted again:

"I don't know why I married a bitch like you!"

The other guests looked embarrassed but said nothing. In a short time, they left promising to come next Thursday. Mrs. Jenkins seemed not to be affected at all by the comportment of her husband, and besides, she was a woman of very quick actions. She called Karl and asked him to pay attention to what she was about to tell him:

"I'll change the security code for the main gate and you'll give a new card to everyone in the house. Mr.

Jenkins is not allowed to put his feet inside the gate and I underline this, *under any circumstances.*"

Karl interrupted her:

"What about his workshop? He comes from time to time and works on his wood sculptures."

"Closed for business and forever. We'll make an extra garage of that place. Tomorrow morning, you'll call a crew of movers with a big truck and they will pack Mr. Jenkins' all his belongings including his toothbrushes. They will also pack all the stuff from his workshop and after they finish, they will take the truck outside the gate and drop everything on the ground. You pay them and they will leave. Then, you call Mr. Jenkins and tell him to come over and pick up his stuff, or otherwise it will be stolen. Make sure that all my instructions will be followed through with precision. Is there everything clear?"

"Perfectly clear, Madame."

In the next morning, Mrs. Jenkins hired the best divorce lawyer in the country who resided in Philadelphia, and flew him first class over to Boston. They spent about six hours in her study with locked doors, going over many papers and making sure that all the details of legal proceedings were thoroughly covered.

Mr. Jenkins came over and picked-up his stuff, but never expected the outcome that followed. He was sued for divorce and his lawyer could not show the ability to present the right arguments for him to win the case. The settlement came all in favor of his wife with a triumphal victory. He got only his wood factory, and only a tiny portion of the entire wealth they both shared.

The family gathered around the kitchen table and every one made comments about that event.

"Now she is going to be more nervous than before", Nancy said.

"No, she won't", Lara said. "She wanted to get rid of him for a long time and only waited for the right time. This was an occasion she couldn't pass and grabbed it with eagerness. I only feel sorry for Suzie, who fell in the middle and doesn't understand probably much of what happened between her parents."

"They both got shared custody of her but Suzie has to go to her father's place if he wants to see her, and only for the weekend", Karl said. "It is a very sad situation for the poor girl."

At home when they were alone, Lara explained to Adam about that delicate situation in which Suzie was compelled to live.

"I'm surprised that you didn't volunteer to adopt her", Adam said.

"I'm not that charitable, my dear son."

The end of the summer was there, the new school year began, and Adam entered the fourth grade. In addition to the regular curriculum, he had German and piano lessons, after classes. When he came home in the first day, he jumped up and down like a little savage, shouting and showing a big joy to his mother.

"I'm no longer the smallest in my class! There are three boys and four girls who are shorter and more slender than I am! This is because I worked so hard on my body the entire summer to make it taller and stronger! Aren't you happy, Mom?"

"Immensely! If you continue with your workout, you'll end up being maybe next year, the tallest, and the strongest in your class! We'll go this Saturday and buy new clothes for you because these became too small."

"I'm going to the kitchen and tell everybody!"

He rushed to the kitchen where the entire family was there, and told them with loud voice about his formidable performance. His face was radiating and his words sprang of his mouth like in a race to get out first. They all surrounded him and embraced him with warmth, when Mrs. Jenkins showed up.

"What is going up? I heard a lot of noise."

"Adam is no longer the smallest in his class", Aki said.

"Is that so? What is your secret?"

"I worked out very hard all the summer, Madame, to make my body taller and stronger. Uncle Aki helped me a lot in the gym and with Karate lessons. I also swam a lot almost every day. My mother said that all my hard work paid off, and I'm very happy. We'll go this Saturday to the city and she we'll buy me new clothes because these became too small for me."

"Don't bother Madame with your peroration, Adam", Sharon said.

"I'm very sorry, Madame, if I annoyed you. Have I caused any trouble?"

"No, Adam you didn't cause any trouble. I'm happy

for you, and I advise you to continue with your workout and become even taller and stronger."

"Thank you, Madame, that's what my mother advised me too."

"She did, didn't she?" ("What a marvel this boy can be", she thought).

In the coming Saturday they went to the city and Lara let him choose the clothes he wanted. He picked the cheapest and the less fashionable.

"Is this what you want? They don't look attractive to me at all."

"This is what all the boys wear in my class. I don't want to be different."

Lara shrugged and let him have what he wanted.

"Next week", she said, "your birthday is coming and you'll be officially eight years old. Would you like something special to have or to do? Just ask."

"No, thank you, Mom. I have everything I need and I don't see any special way to celebrate it. I rather like to stay home with you, read, and listen to music."

"I tell you what we can do. We can go ice-skating to 'Steriti Rink', which is an indoor ice rink with harbor views, and we can have a nice dinner there. What do you say?"

"Sounds good to me, but I don't know how to skate and I don't have skates, but we can go and watch the others and look at the ships in the harbor. Dou you know how to skate?"

"Just enough to keep standing on my feet without falling. Come, we'll buy skates and boots for both, and we'll go next Saturday and have a lot of fun. There is no need to tell the others at home."

In the coming week, Adam started his first piano lesson and was thrilled.

"Mrs. Winston tested my level and asked me to play something. I played *Brahms' Lullaby* reading the notes, and she said that I did great. She gave me lots of exercises to practice but since we don't have a piano at home, I'll do the best I can in school, after hours."

"I'm more than proud of you, especially that you didn't play in a long time. Regarding practice, do the best you can and don't put any stress on you because you cannot perform as you wish. You're not making a career by playing piano."

In those days when he had piano lessons and practice, Lara had to drive over and pick him up from school, since Aki had to stick to Suzie's schedule and make sure of not being late for taking her home.

Mrs. Jenkins found out and told Karl:

"She doesn't have to go and pick up Adam from school. I can tell Aki to do that."

"I don't think she will accept, since it's not part of her job, and she doesn't take anything for granted."

"Can you tell me about her something new beside what I already know, Karl?"

"Nothing that I can think of, Madame."

In the coming Saturday, Lara and Adam went ice-skating as they planned. The arena was crowded but they chose the area for the beginners, where mostly children with parents tried their balance on the ice. They both had the greatest enjoyment, not even expected. Until they could stand up on their feed and slide on the ice, they fell several times, having tremendous laughs, and making fun of each other. When they became tired and had about enough, they had dinner in the restaurant facing the harbor.

"I had not such a great enjoyment in a very long time, Mom."

"Happy Birthday my dearest, and may your life be filled with many even greater enjoyments, every day and at every step on the path of your journey to success."

They embraced each other with deep warmth knowing well that the bond between them was indestructible. Ever since that day, they went many times ice-skating, having always a big pleasure, and finding something new to enjoy.

It was passed ten in that evening when they arrived home, and everybody was asleep. Only one light was on, at the window of Mrs. Jenkins, and she was standing there looking outside. The next morning she called Karl.

"Where were they yesterday and why they came so late night home?"

"They were ice-skating and had dinner at the restaurant facing the harbor."

"Why?"

"Probably, because they wanted to have a good time together. They like talking a lot, mostly in French when they are alone. Does their behavior bother Madame?"

"And if it bothers me, can you or I do something about?"

"No, Madame, we cannot do anything about."

Mrs. Jenkins had too many questions without answers swirling in her mind.

One evening close to dinner time, she was at the table alone, waiting for Suzie to join her.

"She is not coming to dinner, Madame", Karl said. Suzie said that she is not hungry, and you should have dinner alone."

"I'm going to see what caprice she has now."

Suzie was sitting on her bed reading a book, when her mother opened the door and said:

"Come to dinner, I don't like eating alone."

"I'm not coming, Mother. (She stopped calling her 'Mommy'.) I want to eat with them in the kitchen and not at your elegant table."

"Are you out of your mind? They are servants and not members of our class."

"They could be, as you said, but they are people alive, they talk a lot, they laugh a lot, they are warm and loving each other. They are my friends, I like them and they like me, with or without your blessing."

"Where did you learn to talk like that?"

"From Adam. He might have a small body but he has a very bright and big mind. He said that everyone should stand up and defend those who cannot defend themselves. Everyone should fight for fairness and justice without being scared by the law or by prejudices. This is exactly what I'm doing now. I defend my friends down there against your preconceived opinions and your unreasonable feelings. I'm growing up, Mother, and you don't even bother to notice."

"I should have guessed that Adam had something to do with your strange behavior. Have it your way."

She turned around and left, with her mind full of particular moments that she will never forget: *"Those are mature stories and I'm too young for understanding them. When I'll grow up I'll be mature and then I'll read them, and I'll absorb every word with all the pores of my well trained mind. My mom is very mature, Madame, and she understands everything."*

That little boy with *a small body and a very bright and big mind,* as Suzie so well described him, was no less than a marvel.

Time went by, month after month, year after year, leaving behind precious memories to be remembered and treasured. Adam was already fourteen years old and finished the tenth grade first in class like every year before. He worked so hard on his body that he became the strongest and tallest in his class even if he was three years younger than his classmates were.

One day, Lara approached with caution the subject of puberty.

"Nothing to worry about, Mom. Uncle Karl and Uncle Aki, taught me everything about this subject. They taught me how to handle the most sensitive exposure that I have to encounter in my stage of adolescence. They also will show me later how to shave my moustache that started growing. When it will become thicker, I intend to let it grow and also I'll like to have growing a small goatee beard."

"I can breathe easier now. It was a subject that I had no idea where to start talking to you about. I can spot a shade of your moustache and this makes me think that you're not a child anymore, and I'm getting older."

She made a long pause and continued:

"I would like to ask if you thought about what career you intend to take up. Do you have a particular vocation that you like to pursue?"

"Professor of International Law. I speak French, German, Japanese, English American, British, and Eastern New England English, and I don't want to waste my knowledge by being a simple lawyer."

"Wow! How did you come up with such a distinguished profession?"

"Remember the captain who let us go free?"

"How can I ever forget him? He saved our lives."

"He told me then: 'You'll make a fine lawyer when you'll grow up'. His words were embedded in my brain ever since and I nestled them as a precious treasure. I thought about his words many times and I had no doubts that becoming a lawyer was my destiny. Not only that, but I want to be a Professor of Law, to teach the young generation how to think and evolve rationally."

"Sometimes, I have no words to express my amazement when you talk. You have my blessing and all my support for the marvelous projects you want to achieve."

Tears started flowing down her cheeks, but she

didn't bother to wipe them. Adam embraced her with warmth and understanding thinking that she sacrificed her life and made possible for him to reach everything he loved to achieve.

"I have to tell you something that I also nestled for a long time in my brain: When you'll graduate from high school and you'll enroll to college, we have to move out from here and have our own place. I thought that by then, after ten years, the statute of limitation will be over, and I don't have to be worried anymore. After that, I consider to have plastic surgery and have my face restored to its original features. More over, after that I want to apply for being reinstated in my position of professor at the university. In the past years, I studied a lot to take the examination for passing the test with big confidence."

"Now it's my turn to not have words enough for expressing my feelings and my thoughts! You just gave me the only piece in my jigsaw puzzle that was missing and I needed to win the entire happiness of my life! I don't know if I'm dreaming or if what you just told me is for real!"

"I told you what I want to do, and it's in my mind from a very long time. We have to work together everything we want to achieve."

"Now it's my turn to say: You have my blessing and all my support for the marvelous projects you want to achieve."

They both felt like a gate opened before them and a light of tremendous brightness invited them to step in.

One day at a weekly bridge party of Mrs. Jenkins, while Lara was busy in the kitchen arranging the trays with snacks, a man entered and asked for a glass of water.

"They have all kind of drinks there," he said," but no water. May I have one glass, please?"

He was tall with an athletic body, about forty years old or even younger, very handsome, had wavy auburn hair, hazel eyes, fair complexion, and a beautiful smile. He was stunned when noticing Lara's face; he came closer to her and said:

"Forgive me if I'm intruding, but have you ever considered a plastic surgery to restore your face? My name is Thad Barlos and I am a physician at the Research Institute of Reconstructive Surgery. My specialty is craniofacial surgery and I can help you."

"Thank you for your kindness Doctor Barlos, but I cannot afford the cost of a surgery to reconstruct my face."

"We introduced at the Institute a new method of chirurgical procedure that is in experimental stage and we need volunteers who will permit us to test every step of the operation. Would you be interested?"

"I might, but first I have to ask which will be my best and worst chances?"

"The best will be that your face will be completely restored at its original features. The worst will be that your face will remain the same as it is."

"Thank you again for your kindness Doctor Barlos, but I need more time to think about."

"Here is my card and call me when you're ready. I perform miracles!"

Lara decided to call him, but only after she will finish with everything else she had to do.

Two more years passed, Adam graduated with honor from high school, and only at sixteen, he applied to one of the best universities in the city for becoming a lawyer. He was accepted with the highest grade, above all the other contenders to start his first year of studying for his BA degree. It was time for them to move out.

"I called a real estate broker to find a house for us in the suburbs", Lara told him, "and as soon as he will find one that we like, I'll make the down payment to buy it, we start packing the little belongings we have, and we go."

They looked at three houses found by the broker but didn't like any of them. In the coming week, he showed them exactly what they needed: a two stories house with a deck upstairs, three bedrooms, two bathrooms, a small garden, and a garage, located in a nice area in the suburbs. Lara signed all the papers and they were ready to move in.

"I have to give a week notice to Mrs. Jenkins, tell the family, and in the meantime we'll go and shop for furniture and everything we need in our household."

"I'm coming with you", Adam said.

They knocked at the study door and entered after having permission from Mrs. Jenkins.

Lara armed herself with all the courage needed to confront a tempest, and told Mrs. Jenkins the story she was not a bit prepared to hear. She listened with calm to what Lara had to tell her, and said:

"I knew that this will come one day, and I wish you both the very best of luck. Find another maid to replace you, if you are eager to go!"

"Madame", Adam said, "I wish to thank you from us both, for all the kindness and the good will you showed us for the past ten years, and for the opportunity you gave us to have a home and a family. We'll treasure the time we lived in your house and we'll cherish the memories we are taking with us."

He bowed and kissed her hand, smiling in the same time.

"You are a better person than your mother, Adam. Much, much better. I'm glad I knew you. Maybe sometime you'll come and see me. Good bye to you both."

Lara expected a rude encounter, but not such a cold and hostile one given to her. She was happy anyway, that everything went without a major confrontation, and they both left the room. Downstairs, Adam already told before, to everybody about their leaving, and they tried by turn to show them their regret and sadness.

"As soon as we settle into our home, I'll let you know, and you can come over anytime to visit us", Lara said.

She called Greta and asked for a maid to be sent over to serve Mrs. Jenkins.

"You are giving me another headache, Lara. Where can I find one, especially to be permanent on the job?"

"Take an aspirin and please find a maid for her, or I'll be not able to move out. You have one week, and please hurry up."

Lara and Adam decided to postpone the purchase of what they needed for their home, until they will move in and had plenty of time. One day before her notice expired, the new maid came over and Lara showed her around. She was middle aged, had slow movements and talked a lot. As soon as Lara gave her the initiation for the job, she rushed to the dwelling that was their home for about ten years. Adam started already packing and Lara joined him until late night when they finished. All their belongings fit in their little car and they didn't need any help from the family. In the morning, they went to make their farewells to the people who were their best friends, and the only family they had, promising each others to stay in touch. Late night when she went to bed, Mrs. Jenkins found a small envelope on her pillow with only one word written: "Patricia". She opened it and inside was a small card showing on the front a picture of a raindrop hanging from a dry leaf. Inside the card she read: *"As time goes by, it leaves behind only very few dear moments to be remembered and cherished."* There was no signature. Mrs. Jenkins became stunned at first, and then she burst into a deep sobbing that seemed without end. Only once in her life she cried like that when she was very young and her sister died.

Nobody knew at that time, as nobody knew it now. Only Lara knew, because she wanted her to cry, and she made her sobbing. *The Little Prince* in the story had his last tinkling laughter before he returned to his planet.

CHAPTER 3

Gliding Steps

Lara and Adam arrived to their owned house before noon, and after unloading the car, they started looking around and decided for everything they needed to buy. Without wasting any time, they went to the city, chose the furniture including a standard size piano, and bought all the supplies needed in their household.

The truck with the stuff came early in the evening and all the furniture was set in the right place. Lara started to arrange in a proper order the small items especially in the bedrooms and kitchen, waiting for Adam to help her, but as if he didn't have anything better to do, he started playing piano, entertaining himself with Liszt's *Piano Concerto No.1.*

"Adam! Come and help, or you'll sleep on the floor!"

"Mom, I'm so happy that I could sleep on the ground outside or on the top of the roof!"

"Go to the study and arrange the books and the music collection on the shelves!"

"They are not going anywhere, Mom. Tomorrow

they will be in the same place and I'll arrange them with pleasure, wherever you like."

Lara smiled, thinking that she was no less happy than her son was, but somebody had to do the job, and she was the only one available at that time. Finally, he came over only because he was hungry.

"The fridge is full, take whatever you like and make me a sandwich too. I think I did enough for today, it's almost midnight, and we'll go to sleep."

In the next morning after breakfast, they both were ready to work in the study.

"Which one is my desk?", Adam asked.

"The one you like and the other one is mine."

After finishing the arrangement of the books and music collection in the right places on shelves, Adam said:

"I have lot to study this summer before the school year begins, and I might need some books."

"What might be the subjects of your study since you don't even know what courses you'll take."

"Oh, but I know my dear Mom. I'll tell you what my plan is, if you're curious to find out."

"I can barely wait to find out. Tell me all."

"To becoming an International Lawyer, first I have to complete an Undergraduate Degree Program to get a BA, but I don't want to spent four years just taking courses that later I don' use. There are opportunities to study international law at the undergraduate level through a legal studies or an interdisciplinary law bachelor's degree program. Students may pursue the international arena by taking core courses on legal system structure and elective classes to specialize. The other classes I intend to take will be Arts and Humanities, Social Science, and Philosophy. You see, in this way I shorten the time for studying Law, later when I'll attend the Graduate School to earn the Juris Doctor degree for which I need a three-year, full-time academic program and which is required for practicing law. After that, I'll be eligible to sit for the bar examination. If I want to teach Law, I'll have to take a one-year degree program for my Master of Laws degree. For this achievement are considered only applicants who excelled in their basic law school studies. I can skip this level and apply directly to 'Doctor of Juridical Science', which is the highest form of law degree, is equivalent to PhD, and can be finished in three years as a full time student. This program will qualify me to work as Law Professor in academic settings."

He made a long pause and asked:

"What do you think, Mom?"

"It's good that I was sitting down, or otherwise I would have fainted. In simple words, I'm astounded."

Adam came close to her, kissed her both hands, and caressed her hair:

"I only can do all these, because you sacrificed your life for me and gave me the chance to grow up having everything I needed for my education."

Lara wiped her tears and said:

"Let's go buy books for you and for me."

They spent a lot of time in the bookstore and bought everything they needed.

"I want some paintings to hang on our bear walls, to make our house more familiar", Lara said.

"You spent a lot of money lately. Maybe we can live without paintings for a while."

"We still have plenty of money, and I'm going to tell you how we stand. In the past ten years, I saved all my salary money, and I have quite a bit of money from before. Your account comes good too and is growing. I was thinking to buy a new car and keep this one for you when you'll have your license and start driving. What do you say?"

"You are amazing me as always. If I wouldn't be so big, I would start jumping up and down. Let's go buy the paintings you want."

They went to an art gallery and bought some good copies of *Turner, Aivazovski, Dürer,* and impressionist painters.

Back home, they spent a lot of time arranging everything in the right place, and Lara said:

"The statute of limitation is over for us, and we don't have to be scared anymore of being hunted. We are free and we can show everywhere in public without looking over our shoulder. Maybe we should celebrate our freedom any way you like."

"I want to have my name back. How can I do that? I want to be called *Adam Justin Collins.*

"This is a great idea! I'll change mine too and I'll like to be called *Lara Andrea Collins.* Let's go to court and file a petition to legally change our names. We'll go tomorrow morning and after that we'll go and buy a new car."

The next morning they did just that. They filed a petition with the court clerk and had to be in court for the hearing with the judge in the next day. They returned home, left the car, and went back to the city by bus, to buy a new one. A small and beautiful car was chosen by Adam, and Lara agreed that it was exactly what they needed.

In the next day they were due in court, and after listening to their request, the judge signed the *Decree Changing Name* for both and they got a certified copy from the court clerk to be used for changing all their documents.

"I would very much like to get my driving license, since I am at the right age and I have a car."

"Hit the book and learn, and because of your age, you need to attend the driving school. When you're ready we'll go to the right place and you'll take your test. In the meantime we'll do some driving around to make sure that you can be confident and pass the test."

After three weeks, Adam got his driver license.

"I would like to go and see our family. Would you like to join me?"

"No."

"Just like that? May I ask why?"

"I don't go there. I've spent ten years like a slave in that house and I have enough. You go and ask them to come over and see me if they want. Don't stay long."

Adam went to pay a visit to the family. They were thrilled to see him and listening to everything he told them about what happened since they left. He asked them to come over and see his mother and the beautiful house they have; they promised to come in the coming Saturday.

Lara prepared a feast, cooking a lot and making sure that all of them in the family will have what they like most. They all came in that Saturday morning, and each wanted to speak first, about their amazement after visiting the house and seeing how beautiful everything was. Lara told them some of what they achieved lately, and she thought that it was the right time for them to know who she was and where she came from. All of them were stunned after listening to her story.

"I intend to have surgery one of these days and restore my face. After that, I'll apply to be reinstated in my position of teaching at the university."

"I feel like I'm dreaming", Sharon said.

"I feel like I just stepped into something illusory, into a world of miracles", Nancy said.

"When I saw your picture back there on Adam's desk, I assumed only that you had a past which was not to be disclosed, but never expected to be like that", Karl said.

"I'm amazed too, like the others, but I love you and Adam, no matter who you are and how your face looks", Aki said.

"I must thank you all, and I hope you understand now why I was unable to tell you the truth for so many years. My dearest wish is that you all will be always close to me and Adam, like before, and keep us both in your family that we love and treasure."

They all felt tears coming in their eyes, and embraced each other with warmth and love. It was Lara's turn to ask about Mrs. Jenkins and Suzie.

"It will be hard for you to believe, maybe, but she is dating Doctor Maurs. They are about the same age, divorced, and like fit for each other", Karl said.

Lara had a big laugh. The others joined her.

"She stopped firing the maids who came one after the other. Now there is none in her service, and we do by turn a lousy job to clean the house, but she doesn't care to notice", Sharon said, "Monday we'll expect another one to come and we'll see how long she will last."

"About Suzie", Nancy said, "she applied to college for studying business, because her mother chose her career, since she will inherit a fortune and she has to know how to manage it."

"Poor girl", Lara said, "how little her mother knows her and how far from each other they are!"

It was almost late evening when they left, promising to come again. In the next day, Lara told Adam that she intended to have surgery as she planned.

"I'm with you all the way, even if I'm worried like never before in my life", Adam said with a trembling voice.

Lara didn't tell him how scared she was. She called Doctor Barlos and made an appointment for the next day. Adam went with her and like walking on thorns, they both entered the doctor's office. He was smiling and showing contentment to see Lara.

"This is my son Adam", she said,"he wanted to be with me."

"I'm very glad that you decided to have surgery", the doctor said. "I'm pleased to meet you Adam, and I assure you that your mother will be fine and there is nothing to worry about. Now have a seat there, and you Mrs. Collins please come over and sit on this chair."

For more than one hour, he checked Lara's face, taking pictures from all sides and corners, and talking only to the nurse who helped him. After he finished, he said:

"I'll schedule your operation for this Thursday, if this is convenient for you."

"Yes it is, and the sooner the better."

"Very well then, Thursday at seven please be here. Let me tell you about the procedure, such that you'll know all the stages, one after the other. First, I'll work on the bony injuries of your nose which was severely broken. Secondly, I'll operate on your right eye, which was narrowed by the injury that fortunately has not affected your vision. Third, I'll make a thorough check on special regions of your face that encompasses the nerves in your face. Fourth, I'll work on each scar and I'll smooth every bit of it. You will spend the first two days after surgery in the intensive care unit. If you do not have a complication, you will be able to leave the hospital within one week. Bandaging will be removed after the fourth post-op day. The new procedure is using polarized laser whose action works to stimulate growth of new collagen fibers and the new skin that forms is smoother and firmer. There will be no suture to remove after surgery. With these new procedures, complete healing may take about two weeks after which, there will not remain the faintest trace of the surgery that could be detected even under the most powerful magnifier. The operation including treatment for the entire period of your stay in the hospital, will cost you nothing. If you have questions please free to ask."

"Do I have to expect pain or a big discomfort?"

"You will have to take some medication for mild pain if you feel like. At the end of the first week and the beginning of the second week, you may feel a little blue or depressed. This common reaction to surgery is transient. In the next few days, as the bruising fades, the swelling subsides, and you resume your normal life, a sense of elation replaces the down feeling. This 'blue' feeling may occur even though you have read about it and tried to avoid it. Anything else?"

"No, Doctor Barlos. Even if I'm scared, I'm glad I decided to have this operation. Thank you for explaining me everything and I'll be here Thursday at seven sharp."

On the way back home, both Lara and Adam showed very little enthusiasm for this new occurrence in their life. For the next couple of days, Lara followed all the instructions given to her, and Adam made sure that she will not skip any of them.

"I'm not your baby, Adam. You don't have to look over my shoulder all the time. I'm doing just fine."

"I want to make sure that you obey what the doctor said and be ready for surgery. I'm going to call Uncle Karl and ask one of the family to come over and stay with me at the hospital for as long as the operation will be."

Lara had no objection and thought that indeed will be better for Adam not to be alone in those moments. Thursday morning at seven, they both went to the Institute. A nurse came over, asked Adam to stay in the waiting room, and took Lara with her. After few minutes, the entire family showed up and ready to wait there even for the entire day.

"Mrs. Jenkins will reprimand you all for such disobedience", Adam said.

"We told her where we're going. First she was stunned, then she made a barely audible sound, and after that we don't know what she did, because we left", Karl said, and then he started pacing the floor.

After more than five hours, Doctor Barlos came to the waiting room and said to Adam:

"Your mother is doing fine; she is in the intensive care unit where she will be for the following two days. It will take her a little while until she wakes up, but you cannot see her until she will be moved to a regular room. These are precautions we have to take in this stage after surgery, to avoid any complications that might occur from an unsterilized medium coming from outside. You can go home and rest because you look like you are about to faint. Come tomorrow just to ask how she is, or if you prefer, call me and I'll be glad to tell you. Do you have anybody at home?"

"This is my family and one of them will be glad to stay with me. Thank you Doctor, and I'll be here first thing in the morning."

Aki was eager to stay home with Adam and spend a good time with him especially talking Japanese. The others went back to the house and promised to come after two days when they will be allowed to see Lara. The next morning, Adam went to the hospital and asked for Doctor Barlos. He was in surgery but a nurse came over and told him that his mother was in very good spirit and was doing unexpectedly good.

"Tomorrow", she said, "you can come in the afternoon and see her. Her first word when she woke up was 'Adam'. Go home now, because there is nothing you can do, by sitting in that chair."

"I'll stay for a while. I brought a book with me and I'll keep myself busy. If there are any changes, please let me know."

The waiting area was a quiet and private environment where snacks and beverages were available, as well as computers and video games.

Adam was alone and kept reading his book when Doctor Barlos showed up.

"Why don't you go home, Adam? The nurse told you that only tomorrow you could see your mother. She is doing very well. You look tired and worried. If you cannot trust a doctor like me, you'll not make a good doctor. How old are you?"

"I'm going to be a lawyer, not a doctor. I'm sixteen."

"Oh, you still have two more years of high school to decide about a career."

"I'm going to college this fall, and I decided long ago to become a lawyer."

"This is very interesting. I'm really amazed. Now, go home, rest, and have something to eat. I'll see you tomorrow afternoon."

In the evening, Aki called:

"I won't be able to come and stay with you tonight, because Madame goes out sometime this evening with Doctor Maurs and she might need me. You come over and stay with Nancy and me, since we have plenty of room."

"I'll be there around seven, Uncle Aki."

Adam drove there and found the entire family in the kitchen. Suzie was there too. They all started to have a nice chat when Mrs. Jenkins showed up.

"What are you doing here? Where is your mother?"

"In the intensive care. I couldn't stay home alone and Uncle Aki asked me to come over and spend the night here with him and Auntie Nancy."

"So now you're a baby without your mother?"

A blind rage came to Adam's face and he felt like exploding, but he only made a long pause and said with a soft voice:

"I cannot answer to your question Madame, I really cannot."

"Give him something to eat. He looks like he is starved", she said. "Suzie, come to dinner!"

"I'll come later, Mother. Now, I want to spend some time with Adam and my friends here. You go ahead and have your dinner."

Without another word, Mrs. Jenkins turned around and left.

"I think it's better for you to go, Suzie", Karl said. "Your mother will get angry and she will reprimand us and not you."

"Maybe you're right. I'll go. Good night everybody."

Adam spent the night there and early in the morning, he went home. In the few hours until afternoon, he tried to read, but his mind was concerned only about his mother. Close to three o'clock, he drove to the hospital, and met with the entire family who already was there. A nurse approached them and said that they were allowed to visit Lara, but only for ten minutes and touching her was not permitted. Adam entered first in the room and saw his mother with all her head bandaged and, only her left eye and her mouth were uncovered. She smiled showing her impeccable pearl-like teeth.

"Hi, dearest", she said. "I missed you all the time."

"Me too my dearest Mom. I was worried and scared. Now that I can see you and talk to you I feel more easy. How are you doing? Doctor Barlos said that in a few days you can come home."

"I feel great and curious about my look, but it cannot be worse than before, and this is a comforting thought."

The others approached and every one said a few words and showed big concern for her. When time for leaving was close, Doctor Barlos showed up.

"She is doing better than I expected. A very mild pain she has and gets medication for it; she has no complication, which was my main concern after surgery. The day after tomorrow I'll remove the bandages and after two more days she can go home. You'll be surprised when you'll see her face. Maybe, I'll be too."

After a few minutes, the nurse came and said that the visit time was over. The family said goodbye and left while Adam said to her before leaving:

"I'll be here tomorrow morning, Mom. Don't go anywhere, please."

Lara smiled and told him to behave. In that night, Adam stayed home alone and felt relaxed and much better. The next afternoon he drove to the hospital and went to Lara's room without asking any permission this time. He was still very cautious not to come too close to her and not to touch her hands as he wished. He told her everything what happened since her operation, and especially how enraged he was by Mrs. Jenkins' attitude and how much he would have liked to punch her in the nose. Lara had a laugh and was very amused, imagining the whole scene.

"Mom, tomorrow is the big day and I'll be here next to you when Doctor Barlos will take off your bandages. Remember last time when the doctor took off your bandages and asked me to touch gently your scars? Only this time will be for a different reason."

"How can I forget? You were so young and so scared! After so many years we have to live the same scenario, only as you said, for a different reason."

The nurse showed up and asked Adam to leave and come tomorrow by nine o'clock for the big event.

The next morning, Adam was at the hospital before seven o'clock and not taking a seat in the waiting area, but standing next to the door of his mother's room. Doctors and nurses passed by, without paying any attention to him. Finally, Doctor Barlos showed up close to nine o'clock and Adam said:

"I would like to stay next to my mother when you'll take her bandages off."

"Why, if I may ask? Any special reason?"

"Yes Doctor, a very special one." He told him the exact reason.

"You are an outstanding young man, Adam. Come in and the nurse will give you a medical coat and a seat next to your mother."

"Are you ready, Lara? I'm about to unveil my *Galatea.*"

"As ready as I can be, Doctor *Pygmalion.*"

Adam sat next to her keeping her hands that were trembling no less than his ones. The doctor started to take the bandages off her head, with very slow motions until the last piece. Adam stared at his mother with his mouth wide open.

"Adam close your mouth or you'll catch a fly. Just find your voice and say something."

"Welcome back Andrea", Adam whispered.

The nurse came with a big mirror and gave it to her. She stared at the image in the mirror and opened her mouth to say something but no sound came out.

"Close your mouth, Lara, I don't want to treat you for sour throat."

She repeated Adam's words:

"Welcome back, Andrea."

Except for a few minor bruises and small swellings, everything was perfect. Her face was exactly like she had it long time ago. Heavy tears came to her eyes and Adam joined her in a short crying.

"I told you that I perform miracles", the doctor said "you don't need any make-up."

"I never wore make-up in my life."

"I could let you go home, but I prefer to keep you here for two more days and watch the entire healing process. You can walk around the room and even outside on the corridor, to stretch out your legs. Adam can accompany you, and then go eat something or I have to give him artificial nourishment. I have to leave you now because I have other patients waiting for me."

He left without waiting for them to thank him. Adam walked with his mother as the doctor said, until she became tired and went back to bed.

"Go home my dear, I need to rest, and I'll be here tomorrow waiting for you to have us both a nice chat and a refreshing walk outside this room. There is no need to tell the family now. They'll come to see me when I'll be home."

Adam came the next morning and they had a long chat and a walking on the deck outside.

"I think your face is the most beautiful in the world."

"I think that you are my son and your opinion is subjective."

"Oh, yeah? Let's see what other people say!"

A middle-aged man passed by them, and Adam said:

"Pardon me for intruding, Sir, but could you please tell me your opinion about the face of this woman?"

The man looked with big attention at Lara's face and said:

"I've never seen a more beautiful face in my entire life. Indeed, she is amazingly beautiful."

"Thank you very much for your opinion, Sir. She is my mother."

"You, young man, resemble very much to her."

"What are you saying now, my dear Mother?"

"I'm not saying that I'm pleased. I'm saying that I'm thrilled! I can't wait to go home!"

After two more days, Doctor Barlos allowed Lara to leave the hospital, asking her to come back in one week.

She was more than happy when she was home and could touch every thing around as if she was away for a long time.

"My next step", she said, "is to find out the exact processing of my reinstatement in my position of teaching at the university. I made lots of research in this problem and first I have to contact Dean Duncan from my former place."

"What are you waiting for? Just give him a call and start talking!"

In the same day, Lara called Dean Duncan, and after

a long explanation about her life for the past years, she told him what she needed: the records of her profession and all the publications she made as professor. The Dean assured her of all his support and said that as soon as he will be asked by the person in charge with her interview, he will comply with all the requests.

"Which chances do you have?", Adam asked.

"I don't really know. I published many papers, which had a very good reception in the literary community, I had a very good record of teaching, and I have a PhD, which counts the most and opens many doors for me. Next week I'll make an appointment for the interview."

The time for visiting Doctor Barlos came by, and both Lara and Adam went to the Institute. He looked at her face and gave her a big magnifier to inspect every single trace of the operation. Lara couldn't find any. Her face was perfect. He took many pictures from every angle and every side.

"I'll put some of them in my 'Hall of Fame' display. I'll give you too, a couple with dedication, and I'll give you also the picture of your face before the operation. That one, hide it in your desk drawer, and when you look at it, remember only me, and nothing else."

"Thank you Doctor Barlos for everything you did for me. I feel indeed, resembling Pygmalion's *Galatea* who came to life after he crafted her sculpture like a miracle of his art. Thank you Doctor Pygmalion."

He took a very long look at her, asking himself who really that woman was.

"Welcome to life, *Galatea.*"

Lara and Adam went home. In the next few days, Lara prepared lots of notes for the interview, and after one week, she made an appointment with the Dean of Arts and Humanities at one of the highest universities in the city.

"Would you like me to come with you?"

"No. This is my show and I have to play it alone."

Lara went to the office of the Dean and was invited inside. It was a luxurious room and behind a desk, a woman stood up and greeted Lara with a smile. She was in her fifties, very skinny, had a tired looking face, dyed blond hair, and she was limping.

"Good morning, I am Lara Collins."

"I am Professor Magda Taylor, Dean of Arts and Humanities. Good morning Mrs. Collins. I understood from your request for the interview that you want to talk with me about your reinstatement in the position of professor. Tell me all about."

Lara told her everything. The interview lasted almost two hours. After a long pause, the Dean said:

"Your ample description of your situation is very impressive, Mrs. Collins. I shall tell you what I am going to do. I will call Dean Duncan and ask for all your records, and then I will set a meeting with members of the faculty and review thoroughly all of them. I shall give you a call in a few days, and let you know about the decision we took. Goodbye Mrs. Collins, it was a pleasure to meet you."

"Thank you Dean Taylor for seeing me. Goodbye."

Lara went home and told Adam everything in

smallest details. After one week, Dean Taylor called and asked Lara to come in the next morning.

"Are you scared?", Adam asked.

"What do you think that I'm going to a party? Yes, I'm scared. On the other hand, if I don't meet the requirements they will ask for, I always can apply for a teaching position at high school level and certainly I'll be admitted."

The next morning Lara went to the Dean office where three members of the faculty were there. She made all the presentations and said:

"Have a seat, Mrs. Collins. We have reviewed all your records and found them quite impressive. Your PhD thesis is remarkable. We are inclined to reinstate your position, but first, you have to give an one-hour seminar, which will be attended by faculty members, students, and general public. With this seminar, you have to demonstrate the impact of your profession on the highest level of education you have done, and show that you are an outstanding teacher. Members of the faculty will ask you questions of general interest and you'll show that you are a good communicator. The seminar will be held two days from now, at ten o'clock in the morning in the main auditorium. If you succeed, you will be reinstated as Assistant Professor and you will start teaching this fall. Goodbye Mrs. Collins."

Lara went outside feeling dizzy and looking for a chair to sit down and regain her breath. After a while, she went home and talked so fast that Adam barely could make her slow down.

"I have to prepare for the seminar."

Lara went to the study and all day long, she read from books and made notes. In that night, she barely slept a few hours.

In that decisive morning, she dressed up like for a conference, combed her hair pulled back neatly in a bun at the nape, checked thoroughly her getup, and was ready to go.

"Think about me, Adam, and raise your highest hopes. I'll see you later and I'll tell you everything no matter how the outcome will be."

"You'll be at the most of your performance, Mom."

At ten o'clock sharp, Lara entered the auditorium without any papers or material to help her dissertation. The auditorium was packed to-the-gunnels. In the first raw, deans from different departments and members of faculty were already sitting and waiting to find out what that new candidate had to show. After a short greeting, Lara started her dissertation, with a strong and confident voice. In the next hour, she showed them a tremendous knowledge about multiple subjects referred to the course of her studies, gliding-like, her words along her vision of topics for future research in educating the young generation. In the first thirty minutes, she spoke in English. A few times she paced the podium back and forth, but all the time she looked straight at the audience, from the first to the last raw, as if she addressed each and everyone in the auditorium. For the next thirty minutes, she spoke in French, showing the same fluency as she had in English. In the last thirty minutes after, members of the faculty asked her questions of general interest and she made a tremendous demonstration of a great communicator. During her speech, not a single sound could be heard in the auditorium. When she finished, a moment of silence followed, and then the entire audience erupted in prolonged applauses that crowned her superb lecture. Dean Taylor approached her and said:

"Congratulations Professor Collins. Welcome to the faculty."

"Thank you Dean Taylor, this is my happiest moment I had in a very long time."

Outside, Lara took some time to recover from the big emotions she experienced only after her speech. She was eager to go home and tell Adam about her big success.

"No need, Mom. I was there and I cried, not only for the lecture you gave and which was outstanding, but for the moment of reward that you deserved, and for the merit, pride, and dignity that you restored to yourself. I recorded with my camera the entire seminar and your brilliant success. I'm awfully happy!"

"I think I am too, but I feel like my emotions are somewhere floating in the air. I need a little time to restore my glands' functions, I think."

In that evening, they went out and celebrated their happiness at the most luxurious restaurant in the city.

"In about three weeks from now, we both go to school", Lara said. "Let's have a little discussion about this big event. Your scholarship pays tuition and some expenses. You have three choices and it is up to you to take the decision that it will be the most convenient. You can stay home and save money for food and housing; you can move on campus, live in a dorm, and have everything paid from tuition; or, you can have a room outside the campus, which I pay for, and your tuition will go for school and some left money for you. I'll provide pocket money in any of these cases. Tell me which will be your choice?"

"I would like to move on campus, Mom, and live among people of my generation. I want to know them better, to learn about their goals in life, about their behavior, hobbies, and level of intellect. Also, the library is nearby and I will need to use it all the time. You asked me to make a decision and this is what I want."

"Very well, and I hope you made the right one. I would like to mention though, that you must be careful since every one there comes from a different background, which not always is the best one. Some of the students could be bully, some could be anxious to show physical cogency instead of a mental one, some others are rich and can buy their scores while spending time in parties and gambling. Can you handle them?"

"Look at me, Mom. You think that I am an infant and I could be intimidated? I studied a lot the life on campus with all the examples you just gave me. I know exactly what to expect, and you don't have to worry about this problem which I understand well from every aspect."

"Very well, then you have my blessing. Go now to

the Freshman Dean's Office and ask to be assigned to one of the dorms on campus. You don't need me for that. Now, a different subject: I would like the family to come over this Saturday for lunch. Please be so kind and call them before you go to the campus!"

Adam made the call to the family and spoke to Karl inviting them for Saturday, and then he went to the campus. He was assigned to one dorm close to the library, and his roommate was a freshman who came from Germany. All the information regarding rules and regulations were very strict and were contained in a booklet that had to be clearly understood.

In the next couples of days, Lara spent a lot of time in the kitchen cooking a lot for their guests, while Adam made all the investigations around the campus to become familiar with his new surroundings.

Saturday by noontime, the family arrived and Suzie came too. Adam opened the door and invited them inside. When they saw Lara, no one could make a sound. They all were amazed by her look.

"Just don't stand there like mutes. Say something", she said.

"We can't", Sharon uttered.

"Hello, Lara, would be nice if you say."

"I heard about miracles but never saw one", Nancy said. "Now I can look at one. You look like in a dream."

"May I touch your face, Lara?", Suzie asked.

"No, you may not touch my face, Suzie, but you may kiss it."

Suzie kissed her both cheeks and addressed everybody:

"Her face is real and not a fake! She is a miracle, indeed!"

"This is only half of it", Adam said. "You should know the other half. Tell them, Mom."

"You tell them. You're a better talker than me."

"Well everybody, may I present Assistant Professor of English Literature and French Culture, Lara Andrea Collins, my distinguished and dear Mother."

This time, all of them covered their opened mouths with even bigger amazement. Lara had a short laugh and said:

"Let's go to the dining table and eat. I cooked everybody's favorite dish. Come!"

"After lunch I'll show you the film with the presentation she made in front of a huge audience", Adam said.

"We want to see it now", they all jumped at once.

"Then let's go to the living room and watch. I'll show you only parts of it because is too long, about one and a half hour."

During the presentation, sounds like "oh" and "ah", came as a reaction from every one's astonishment. At the end, Sharon and Nancy cried while Karl and Aki became mute. Suzie said only:

"My mother should see this and maybe she will learn something about people, for a change."

They had a tremendous good time until late evening.

Before living, Adam came with a picture of him and Lara, smiling at each other. Karl took it and said:

"I'll have a nice frame for it and set it in our common place which is the kitchen, to have you both with us all the time."

Lara took a long look at them and said:

"You'll understand now why I never told you who I was and where I came from. I was a fugitive wanted by the police for abducting my son, and if you knew, you all would have been in danger. In case the police would have found me, you all would have been charged with harboring a fugitive and with accessory to a felony crime. Keeping silence I've protected you all."

"Yes, we do understand, Lara. We are happy that we could help you and Adam", Karl said.

They embraced both of them and left.

Summer was over, and time for school came by. In that first day, Lara and Adam went to their separate classes with new visions and hopes for a bright future. He called her late evening:

"I'm so happy Mom, I could explode. I like everything, the teachers, my classmates, the campus, and even the food. My roommate is from Germany, and we speak both English and German. Our room is nicely furnished and I have everything I need. I miss you a lot, but I'll see you Saturday and I'll tell you all about."

Lara could barely say a few words because he was in a hurry to go. In that first night she was alone as never before, but also, she was happy as never before.

Adam came home Friday evening. They gave each

other big hugs, and he lifted her with ease in a pirouette dance around.

"Thank you Mom, and my best teacher I ever had, for everything you've done for me."

"I must say the same. We both helped each other on a very difficult and strenuous path of our lives, and we both succeeded to overcome all the obstacles we encountered. We both are free now to fulfill our dreams and reach the happiness we deserve."

They had a long talk, telling each other about everything they experienced in that week.

"Dean Taylor told me that starting next semester I'll hold the position as full professor because I have special capability and knowledge that should not be wasted. I'll have a big increase of salary, meaning that I'll increase your allowance."

"You always give me a reason to be happy. Our lives made a turn that sometimes makes me think that I'm dreaming and it's not real."

"Many times I think so too."

Christmas was already there, and they wanted the family to come over for celebration. Lara called Karl who said that none of them could come because Mrs. Jenkins organized a big party and they all had to be there. He also said that when Mrs. Jenkins saw their picture for the first time, she emitted a shrill sound, covered her face with both hands, and almost fainted. Then she ordered him to take it away because she said, "I don't want to see those two who showed me only ingratitude for everything I did for them. They never told me who they were and where they came from." Karl responded that "those two" were their family and the picture will stay just where it was. Strangely enough, Mrs. Jenkins took no repressive actions and made no other comments.

Lara and Adam spent the holiday in their beautiful home, without any special activity. Most of the time they read material for the coming semester because they both wanted to be by far the best in their achievements.

One year passed with all their expectations greatly fulfilled. In the next year, Adam took in addition to general education, courses in the sciences and humanities, the core study of legal courses along with electives in his area of interest. Those courses empowered students to be ethical problem-solvers who apply critical thinking, analytical and research skills in legal contexts. His Bachelor of Arts degree will be with a major in Legal Studies.

One day, Lara received a call from Doctor Barlos:

"How is my *Galatea*?"

"Very well, Doctor *Pygmalion*, thank you."

"I would very much like to see you."

"May I ask why?"

"Let's say for both, professional and particular reasons."

"Would you like to come over to my house, maybe this coming Saturday at five?"

"I'll be there."

He came as he said, bringing her a bouquet of yellow

roses. Adam greeted him with a big smile while Lara invited him in the living room.

"You look more than exquisite, Lara, and you grew taller, Adam, since I saw you last time. How is school?"

"Very well, I like it a lot. I'm studying to become a lawyer. Would you like to watch my mother's biggest success of her life?"

"Please Adam", Lara said, "this is not the right moment and maybe it's not even the right thing to do."

"On the contrary, I would like very much, Adam, to know everything which concerns your mother, but first please enlighten me about the subject I'm supposed to watch."

"Very well then, it is my pleasure and honor to present you, Professor of English Literature and French Culture, Lara Andrea Collins, my mother and my best teacher."

It was Doctor's Barlos turn to open his mouth and forgetting to close it.

"We don't have flies here, but anyway, you better close your mouth because I want to start the film. I'll show you only parts of it because it's long and maybe you and Mom have important matters to discuss."

His face became pale and he showed a big emotion.

"You are indeed a big miracle and not only the one I performed on your face. You are much more than I envisaged. May I ask who really you are?"

"I let you have a nice chat because I have to go to the library and study. Good night, Doctor Barlos."

Adam left and Lara told him the entire story of her

life. In all that time, he didn't utter a sound. When she finished he only said:

"I wish I knew you long before."

"If you did, you would have given me a higher consideration than for a maid?"

"I only see a face when I have to operate, and I don't care to whom that face belongs. If I knew by then who you were, it wouldn't have make any difference for me. When I said that I wish I knew you long before, I was referring to twenty years ago and not at a recent time."

It was a friendly atmosphere that allowed them both to know better each other. He left late evening when Adam returned home.

"Good night Doctor Barlos. It was very nice of you to come by and see us."

"Please call me Thad. Good night Adam, grow wisely."

"I'll give you a call from time to time, Lara."

"Please do, Thad, your visit was a real pleasure."

On his way back home, Thad's mind was in a state of extreme agitation. His only passion in life was his profession and the care for his patients who needed craniofacial surgery, and who rewarded his excellent skill with the happiness they showed him. His life was turbulent and without any other satisfaction which usually gives fulfillment and joy. He was married to a woman who was possessive, presumptuous, and had control over his life. She was ready to fight him for anything she assumed to be contrary to her principles, her demands, and her expectations. Thad was not a fighter, rather he was shy, he had a contemplative mind, and over the years, he built his lonely world where he sought solitude and where he was safe. After many years of humiliation and struggling against a hostile atmosphere of ill will and malevolence, he managed to get a divorce, leaving everything behind. He moved to his mother's house, where he had a modest but quiet and serene life. When Lara came under his treatment, they had a few casual conversations of general interest, and he started feeling at ease and comfortable in her company. Slowly, without him being able to explain, a particular sensation of joy and contentment started growing in his heart. She had a soothing voice like a lullaby that touched with its warmth his deep buried wounds in his soul. When she left the hospital, he felt like something dear was taken from him, and from that day he felt missing her even more. It took him quite a long time to decide to call her, since he wasn't sure how she will react, and he was not prepared for a rebuff. When she invited him to her house, he was thrilled. She was there, warm, endearing, beautiful as no one. Her brilliant success impressed him but didn't add any new emotional feelings to those he already had. In that night, he fell asleep with the vision of her image in his mind.

They both were hurt and suffered a lot in the past, and found each other in a secluded world of their own, where they shared their feelings, their thoughts, and their deep understanding. Their love grew slowly, without dramatic emotions, but rather with gliding steps with a smooth, graceful motion, longing for happiness.

Very little Thad told her about his early life. Now and then, only when he felt like talking, he told her small fragments but not like a whole story. He was born in Volos, a coastal port city in Thessaly, Greece, and came to the United States with his mother, when he was about six years old, shortly after his father died. His mother worked as a seamstress in a clothing factory and raised him with not much care for a high education. Most of his learning and schooling, he achieved only by working on and off when he became a teenager and started to support himself. When he decided to become a surgeon, he also became well aware of the enormous difficulties that he will have to encounter. Studying during the day and working during the night, he barely could survive. Loan and tuition helped him a lot but not enough to cover all his expenses. Since the beginning, his mother was against his wish to become a doctor, and therefore, she tried everything to discourage him, including her refusal to give him any further support. She wanted him to make a lot of money in America, return with her back to Greece, buy a fishing fleet, and become a fisherman like his father. The woman he married was far from what he hoped to become for him a partner and a friend. When he divorced her, he felt free and promised to himself not ever to get married again. In spite of all the enormous hardship he encountered, he made a brilliant career, and became renowned for his eminent skill.

Lara never met his mother and she had the feeling that Thad was reluctant to any of her attempts to know her. Nevertheless, Lara was determined to find more about that woman who seemed to be estranged from her son.

"I would like very much to meet your mother. Maybe we can become friends", Lara told him, one day when they had a long walk in the park."

"You wouldn't like her. She is not very sociable."

"She is your mother, and this is all it matters to me."

"If you insist, we'll go tomorrow and you'll meet my mother, but I warned you that she is not a very pleasant person."

The next afternoon they went to his mother's place. It was a nice, small house surrounded by a garden, which looked abandoned. Inside, the furniture was cheap, the carpeting was all worn, and the rooms were all messy. A woman in her sixties, short, with very good looking features, sat on a chair, without bothering to greet her guest. It was Thad's mother who showed her entire displeasure when she saw Lara.

"It is my pleasure to meet you, Mrs. Barlos. My name is Lara Collins.

"I have never invited you Lara Collins, but since you're here, have a seat and Thad will bring some coffee. You came to see if I'll make a good mother-in-law?"

"Not really. I came to meet you like a friend, since Thad told me that you don't have many friends and you might use one."

"Well, he lied as usually. I don't need any friends, especially a woman who tries to lure my son into marriage. I had one like you before and she proved to be nothing else but a pest. Are you one of those?"

"No, I'm not one of those. I love your son very much and I care for him without any intention to lure him in to marriage."

"He doesn't need your love and your care. I am good enough for him, and he doesn't need anybody else."

"Mother, don't you think that Lara deserves more consideration and a more civilized language?"

"What I think is none of your business. I just don't want to have the same experience like the one before. Did you forget what a pest the other one was?"

"Not all women are alike", Lara said "and perhaps you should give me a chance to prove that I'm a good and considerate person, without you making any presumptions that might not be true."

"Are you trying to influence my thinking and my opinions? You'll not be capable to succeed."

"I'm very sorry Mrs. Barlos for the misjudgment you so harshly imposed on me, without knowing anything about who I am and what my feelings for Thad are."

The woman took a long look at Lara and then addressed her son:

"Thad, I decided to return home to Greece and live there with my sister. Book me a flight one of this coming days and I'll be out of your way forever. Goodbye, Lara Collins."

She turned her back and went to the other room.

"Don't tell me that I didn't warn you", Thad said.

"I must recognize that I didn't expect such an

aversive attitude against me. I'm really very sorry for not being able to reach her friendship. Let's go home, my dear."

Lara thought that Patricia Jenkins was an "angel of mercy" compared to that horrible woman.

Back home, they both felt a kind of relief since there was no longer any secret between them.

In the meantime, Adam had a few casual relations without strings attached, hoping that one day he will find his sweetheart to fall in love with, and build a strong bond to last forever.

Time went by, revealing more openly many features of distinctive qualities in the personality of Thad. He showed a lot of kindness, consideration, deference, and a sort of caution that involved much wisdom. Adam and Thad became good friends sharing a lot of knowledge, understanding, and learning from each other many aspects of the human nature. Lara couldn't be more happy.

The big day for Adam came to take the Law School Admission Test (*LSAT)* to be admitted in to law school. It was a four hours examination divided evenly between five multiple-choice sections covering critical reasoning, logic, and reading comprehension, plus one writing sample.

In that day, when he came home, Adam kept talking like without end, telling Lara and Thad about the strenuous time he had and what a big relief he felt when he finished the test. As expectedly, he was admitted with the highest grade. His next step was to attend and graduate from Law School after three years, with Juris Doctor (J.D) degree.

One evening, Lara and Thad were cooking when Adam showed up with his sweetheart. Adam was not easy going when coming to intellect and if he decided to bring home a girl, it meant that she was up to his expectations.

"Mom, Thad, this is Amanda Sarah Easton.

She looked like a teenager doll, with sandy reddish hair, green eyes, beautiful smile, and a few freckles on her fine nose. Overall, she was very pretty, attractive, and very charming.

"Welcome to our home, Amanda", Lara said. "Please make yourself comfortable and don't be scared, I'm not going to dissect you."

They all had a short laugh. Only after exchanging a few phrases, Amanda felt more relaxed and looked very pleased with Lara's way of showing her hospitality. They all participated in a discussion regarding school, grades, careers, and solutions to save the world. Amanda showed a great knowledge about all the subjects involved, mentioning that she studies to become a family lawyer, since she cares a lot for the poor and the weak, and mostly about women and abandoned children. Without being asked, she mentioned about her family. She lived with her grandmother Beatrice, who raised her, and very rarely saw her parents who lived overseas, on a military base. Her father was a colonel in the army, and her mother was a nurse.

Both Lara and Thad liked that girl a lot since the

first beginning. Beyond any doubt, she and Adam were very much in love. When it was time for leaving Amanda said:

"Thank you, Professor Collins, and Doctor Barlos, for receiving me with such a warm and kind welcome. It was a great pleasure meeting you."

"I'm not a professor here, Amanda. Please call me Lara. It was a great joy for me knowing you. I'll be delighted to see you again."

"I join Lara, saying that I'm not a doctor here, and please call me Thad. I'll be more than pleased to see you soon."

"Thank you both very much for your kindness. Please call me Ami. I'll be happy to visit you again, whenever Adam will be kind enough to bring me over."

After a couple of days, Adam asked his mother:

"Well, what do you think about my sweetheart?"

"She is adorable."

"I intend to marry her, after I finish all the schools I need for my doctoral degree, or maybe even before. She is everything I dreamed of, to be my wife, my partner, and my friend."

"I'm going with you all the way, as always."

They came every weekend like a nature of habit. Amy felt for the first time in her life that she had the family she always longed for.

After two more years, they both graduated with honor from Law School with Juris Doctor (J.D) degree.

After both passing the Bar Exam, Ami started her practice as a Family Lawyer. In the same time with practicing law as an international legal professional, Adam continued his studies, to earn his Doctor of Juridical Science Degree *(J.S.D.)* equivalent to PhD for achieving his commitment to a career as International Law Professor in academic settings.

Shortly after, Adam flew to London for his first case abroad, together with a team of three other lawyers. They had to defend an American corporation in dispute with a British firm and Adam had his part of the defense to represent. He submitted a strong defense enough to make win the case with a great success. When he returned home, nobody could stop him from talking about his big performance, which brought him a lot of praise from the Director of the law firm where he worked. He was the youngest lawyer of the team and probably the most knowledgeable.

Both Adam and Ami had big salaries, and they decided to buy a house and move together. They found one at walking distance far from Lara's house, just enough big to accommodate all their needs in a very comfortable surrounding. When they moved in, they looked like coming from another world, showing at every step a sort of happiness that neither of them had before. Lara and Thad helped them with the furniture and all the other amenities to provide them with the most comfort they could have.

The time for them to get married was there. A small ceremony was planned followed by a reception where closest members of family and friends from both sides were invited. Lara organized the wedding celebration to be held in a banquet hall and made sure that everything will be at the highest expectations of hosts and guests alike. Every one came to Lara with a long list, which she had to cut it short, since half of the city seemed to become her guests. Only few were invited to attend the church ceremony. Most of the guest were invited directly to the party. It took her a full day to write and send the invitations, even if Thad helped her a lot.

The big day came and after the completion of the marriage ceremony in a small church, they all, guests and hosts, met in the banquet hall. From the Ami's side, only her grandmother was there. Her parents sent only congratulations with best wishes. Lara's and Adam's family members were all there and took their seats at the long table on the podium, next to Lara and Thad. All the other guests were escorted by waiters to their seats at the round tables on the wide floor. A small orchestra played soft music to please everybody. Lara looked around and couldn't see Mrs. Jenkins.

"She was in the study when we left", Aki said, "and she is not coming."

"Take me to her, Aki."

Lara told Adam with a whispered voice, to start dinner without her, and she left.

The house was all in the dark, and Mrs. Jenkins was in the study listening to a recording player.

"Stay here, Aki. She might say nasty words to me and I intend to do the same."

Lara opened the door large, and stood there. She could hear her own voice narrating a story. Only a dim light was on, making barely visible the face of Mrs. Jenkins who was behind her desk. She turned off the recorder and said:

"You came."

"This is what you wanted."

"I love you, Lara. I always loved you."

"You never loved anyone in your entire adult life, Patricia. You only want to control everybody around you. You never needed me to clean your house or make your bed. You needed me just to be there, waiting for the right moment to crush me, and finally to have control over me. I am the only one in your life who prevented you to reach the world record in the *Guinness Book* to meet the holder of the title for *oppressor of a poor girl,* and make you a winner."

"You lied to me all the time for ten years. I never knew who you were and where did you come from. I hated you for this!"

"Or rather, you love hating, and you hate loving, and you cannot make a distinction, because for you, both are combined into one single feeling which is your passion. This powerful emotion controls your entire life."

Lara repeated to her what she told the family:

"I was a fugitive wanted by the police for abducting my son, and if you knew, you would have been in danger. In case the police would have found me, you would have been charged with harboring a fugitive and with accessory to a felony crime. Keeping silence, I've protected you. Maybe your little wild mind could understand this much. Tell me something. In those ten years you called me by all names that flew through your tormented mind, but never by mine. Why?"

"To punish you."

"This is understandable since it's coming from you. In direct translation, this was your immature reaction to my inhibited behavior."

"It doesn't matter now. I'm used to love you and to hate you. I'll keep them both as I please."

"Now it's too late for expressing feelings, yours, or mine. Come, let's go to my son's wedding. There are a lot of guests there, and everybody is waiting."

Lara stretched her hand, but Patricia didn't touch it. She stood up and went to the door.

"Aki, come and escort Mrs. Jenkins to the car, please."

On the road, none of them uttered a single word.

"She just blew her chance to become more human", Lara said to herself.

Inside the banquet hall, everybody had a wonderful time, talking, laughing, and making new friends. Aki escorted Patricia to the table where Suzie and her boyfriend were sitting, and then he took his place at the table on the podium next to the family. Lara took her seat next to Adam. Her dinner plate was in front of her but she couldn't touch the food. Many thoughts in her mind seemed like having complicated directions to follow, when Adam suddenly stood up and asked for a moment of silence:

"Distinguished guests, honored friends, and dear family, today is the happiest day of my life and I am extremely pleased to share it with you all. Before anyone else I have to address to my beloved and precious bride: Amanda, thank you for taking me as your husband, trusting me, and giving me your love. Thank you for your hopes and faith you put forth to bring the best of me without having any doubts that I will reach your highest expectations."

He kissed her dearly, caressed her face, and continued to address the audience:

"I thank you all for being here today to celebrate the happy moment which brought Amanda and me in a union that will be a bond to last forever. First, I have to address my gratitude to the people who helped me grow up in a safe and wonderful ambience, where I could learn to become a better human being, and to understand better the meaning of compassion, kindness, and generosity. Madame Patricia Jenkins, thank you for the benevolence you showed me since the first beginning when you so graciously received me in your house. My adopted family here, around me, thank you for taking me in as your own and giving me your warmth, your care, and your love. My friends and classmates, thank you for being the best colleagues one can have, especially that I was younger than you all, and less prepared to be at your level of knowing the world around. My teachers along many years of studies, thank you for the many branches of knowledge you opened for me, and taught me at every step how to enhance the capacity of my mind to perceive and understand the human intellect. Finally, I salute you, my Mother, my kindest friend, and my best teacher, I bow before you, with the greatest respect and admiration I can have for the most noble and distinguished human being I've ever knew. *Je t'aime du fond de mon cœur comme aucun autre enfant ne peut aimer sa mère.*"

He bowed before his mother and kissed her hands. She caressed his face with love and tears in her eyes. A huge standing ovation followed for several minutes.

The floor was cleared for dancing and the orchestra played a waltz for the newly wed couple who moved with elegance around the ballroom, and one by one other couples joined them. Lara and Thad showed a big enjoyment when dancing for the first time since they met. After a few pirouettes they changed partners with Adam and Amanda.

"Your speech was amazing", Lara said, "everybody was impressed."

"I was very sincere and I meant every word."

"I know my dearest, I know. What plans you and Ami have for the honeymoon?"

"We decided to stay home and enjoy being together and love our new start as a married couple. There is no other better place."

"I think that is the best for you both."

At almost the end of the party, the orchestra offered to the guests as a memento Boccherini's *Minuetto.* Nobody knew how to dance it, but Adam and Ami took the floor and made the first steps. Thad and Lara joined them. They all felt like stepping toward a bright future, living behind the time, which passed. It was their *Minuet through Time*, a moment to remember and treasure forever. They proved to be marvelous dancers following the music with elegant steps, and giving to the audience a splendid performance. At the end, the four of them joined hands, bowed like on stage, and received a loud round of applauses.

The party lasted until late night, when people started to leave. It was a marvelous time for everybody to enjoy and to remember.

After about one week, Adam came with a strange proposition to be considered by his mother:

"There is one loose end that left part of our story still unsettled. I have to go and punish the monster who almost killed us."

"Have you lost your mind? I put behind everything that we suffered, and I don't want even remember what we have been through, if I have to go further with my life and find my happiness."

"Maybe you Mother, but not me. I'll bring that brute to justice and make him suffer the way he wouldn't even dream. He robbed my life from the years I needed the most to be safe and grow in a peaceful climate without being scared and chased by the police for a crime I never committed. He stole from me the most needed time for learning what every child should experience in his tender age, and later what every teenager needed to approach with confidence his hopes to succeed in his life. He smashed your face and made you a fugitive, scared to death by being hunted every minute by the police, while protecting me with your life, day and night, at every single step we made. He robbed you from your career and made you sacrifice your life by becoming a servant only to provide support for us both. Every single minute you lived with scare and you expected to be caught for the only crime of running away from a monster and for protecting your child of being thrown on the streets. How can you tell me that you put behind all our sufferings and you try not to remember what we have been through, when I know well that the entire past is in your mind all the time without any relief? My dear Mother, I am going to give hell on his knees to that savage brute."

Lara became pale, and only could whisper:

"Have you told Ami?"

"Everything to the minute details. She comes with me, since she is an expert in this matter. We'll take a flight tomorrow and once there, we'll prepare together the lawsuit with the District Attorney. Good night dearest, and sleep well. We'll see you next week."

He came back after more than a week and had a long talk with his mother.

"Amanda filed all charges and I spoke to the District Attorney who assured me that we have a strong case to win. The first hearing is scheduled for two weeks from now, and you will come with us."

"Do I have to?"

"Yes dearest, you have to. You are the victim and the judge will question you. There will be witnesses from the police and the hospital who will testify in your favor."

"Is Mrs. Morris still there?"

"Yes, she is, and she will be delighted to see you and testify in your favor. She looks great after so many years, and she was very happy to see me. I explained to her why we couldn't communicate with her during those past years, and she understood. Now, my dear Mother, I have to go and take care of my clients."

Lara's mind was like a turmoil where her thoughts struggled in a labyrinth trying to find their way out.

After two weeks, two days before the trial, Adam, Amanda, and Lara flew to Santa Barbara. They rented a car and Adam drove to the hotel. The first thing Lara did, was to call Mrs. Morris and asked her to come over.

It was a warm and emotional encounter. Lara told her almost everything that she and Adam went through since they left. Mrs. Morris recounted her part of the life she had during that time, mentioning that she found someone who brought her the happiness she never had before.

The next day in court, all three took their places in front of the judge, who was a woman with a stern face and slow movements. Marc came in, escorted by his lawyer, and took his place on the opposite site. He looked older and his good look was all gone.

Asked by the judge, his lawyer answered to a "not guilty plea" at the arraignment, and the trial was scheduled for the next day.

The jury was selected and the trial began with the case presented by Adam who asked to be designated as second-chair prosecutor. He delivered a very well documented portrayal of *Lara Andrea Collins* as a victim of domestic abuse committed by the defendant, and which resulted in grave physical injuries that disfigured her face. At that moment, Adam showed to the Judge and the Jury, the picture with Lara's disfigured face. Every one in the courtroom made a sound of anger and looked at Marc with indignation.

Adam continued his presentation by recounting in details, the life and struggles of the victim for the ten years following the crime committed by the defendant.

He called *Lara Andrea Collins* to the stand to testify on her behalf. All the questions he asked were meant to reveal her entire ordeal throughout the ten years when she was a fugitive. She gave strong and convincing answers without showing any inconsistency. When the turn of the defense attorney came, most of the questions he asked had little or no relevance to the case. He proved not to be prepared at all to sustain the defense.

Testimonials from the police and from the hospital gave a strong impact to the prosecution, as well as the trustworthy evidence presented by Mrs. Morris.

The lawyer for the defense made a very poor case proving a totally ineffective effort to ease the accusations against his client. It took only half hour to the Jury to find Marc Benson "guilty as charged."

The Judge sentenced him to ten years in prison without parole, which was the maximum penalty within the law for the crime he committed. She also ordered for all his assets to be frozen. In addition, the Judge ordered for the long overdue "child support" payments to become forthwith.

It turned out, that after divorcing Lara shortly after she left, Marc married a rich woman, and before divorcing that one too, he transferred all her money in to his account, making a good life for himself.

Before adjourning the court, the Judge asked Lara:

"Do you like to say anything?"

"Yes, Your Honor."

She turned her face toward Marc and said:

"I cannot forgive you for what you did to me and to *our* child. It is for you to forgive yourself. If you can, it means that you must have particular reasons that remained undisclosed in this courtroom and can be justified only by your conscience. But, if you cannot, it means that a grain of honesty is still buried somewhere in your soul and you'll have plenty of time to bring it to the surface and make it grow. When you'll be satisfied with your new feelings, you'll become a better human being, and you'll be thankful to this court for giving you the punishment that you deserved."

She turned to the Judge and said:

"Thank you, Your Honor."

The Judge asked Marc:

"Do you have anything to say?"

He looked at her with derision and said:

"Nothing."

"Well, you'll have plenty of time to think about something. The court is adjourned!"

At the hotel, Lara and Amanda looked exhausted. Adam kissed them both and said:

"I have to go now to accomplish one more step. You two have a good rest and we'll celebrate the victory when I'll be back."

"You know, Ami, what I think? I wish to give that poor woman all the money that Marc stole from her."

"This is what Adam is doing now, Mom."

He came late in the evening, radiating with joy. Over dinner he told them about what he did, mentioning that he felt an immense relief and had a very good feeling about himself. Both Lara and Ami joined him, saying that it was the right thing to do and that everything they came for was accomplished with great success.

"Did you tell her?", Adam asked Ami.

"No, I waited for a more peaceful moment. I am pregnant, Mom."

Lara jumped from her seat and embraced Ami and Adam in the same time.

"Now, I can say with certainty that I'm the happiest human being in the whole world! I barely can wait to keep my grandchild in my arms!"

All three shared a time that they will always remember and cherish.

Back home, Lara paced the rooms back and forth, thinking at what might have happened if Adam would have lost the case. She thought that Marc would have sued them for slander and they would have ended up with another disaster in their lives. The next time Adam came to see her, he said:

"You had doubt in your mind that I could win, when I opened the case, haven't you?"

"Yes, I had, not one, but many and heavy."

"You see, my dear Mother, I never get involved in a case without being very well prepared. Before anything, I analyze very carefully all the details and make sure that everything in my presentation of the case is covered and there are no vulnerable spots. This way makes me one of the best counselors in town, in spite the fact that I am so young."

"What do you want me to say? That I am immensely proud of you? Yes, I am. That your mode of thinking is above any of my expectations? Yes, it is. That your mind is designed like filigree much better equipped to process information at a higher speed than for most people? Yes, it is. I only doubted you because you opened the case after so many years that could become an impediment to be judged with fairness and accepted by the court without prejudice."

"I understand your side, and I love your honesty. Next time, if there will be one, please trust me and don't have any doubts about my knowledge in the field of bringing to justice people who do bad things. *'Sooner or later punishment comes into their lives without us praying for a just retribution to be applied to them because of the evil they did'.* Remember your own words?"

"Yes, Adam, I remember. Thank you my dear for this edifying conversation. Now, go home to your wife who is waiting for you. Make sure that she gets the right nutrition and keeps all the appointments with her doctor."

After a while, in one weekend, Ami went into labor right in due time. Lara and Thad rushed to the hospital, where Adam was in a state of intense strain, sitting next to Ami and keeping her hand. He talked who knows about what, with a voice that sounded like a broken windmill.

"Take him out of here, or I quit!", the doctor shouted.

Thad presented himself and asked permission to assist, while Lara took Adam by the shoulders and forced him out, without paying attention to his protests.

"Let's have a cup of coffee", she said.

"I have to be there with her and make sure that she is all right."

"No, you don't. She is all right there without you bugging everybody and being in the way of the doctor and nurse doing their job."

He started pacing the floor and mumbling all the time. After about one hour, the doctor came out.

"You became the happy father of a marvelous baby boy, and now you can go inside and see them both."

Adam rushed inside and the nurse put in his arms his baby who indeed was marvelous. Ami was smiling and stretched her arms to get them both close to her.

Adam was unable to make a single sound, being overwhelmed with happiness. Finally, with the baby in his arms he came close to Ami and kissed her tenderly.

"I love you both like you cannot even imagine."

"I can imagine, my dearest. I love you both just the same."

It was Lara's turn to embrace Ami and have the baby in her arms. Even if it was too early to tell, she thought that he had the features of Adam.

They named him *Justin Andrew.*

After a few days, Lara found a live-in very skilled nanny with nursing background, to have the best care for the baby, and teach the new mother about everything she had to know.

Summer was almost there with the coming vacation they all needed after the agitated time they have been through lately. Adam and Ami had their plans mostly to stay home, since Adam had to take care of his studies while Ami had a few clients to represent and also she wanted to be close to her baby. Lara and Thad talked about going somewhere to enjoy a good time together, far from duties and problems.

"Where would you like us to go? I can arrange for my vacation any time you're ready", he said.

"I thought about a place, to visit some cultural heritage sites."

"Name one."

"*Cahokia Mounds.* The ancient city of Cahokia was the cultural, religious, and economic centre of the Mississippian culture and it was the earliest and largest pre-Columbian settlement north of Mexico. It is located in Illinois, which is not far from here. What about your pleasure?"

"I thought about something with a more archeological

accent, like *Mesa Verde National Park* in Colorado. I read about this site long ago and I planned to visit it but never had the time. Starting circa 7500 BC, Mesa Verde was seasonally inhabited by a group of nomadic Paleo-Indians known as Ancestral Pueblo people. What do you say?"

"My vacation starts next week, and you can arrange for yours. Let's go there and have the best time we ever had together."

They booked a package trip with best hotel, rented car, guide tours, and all the other accommodations included. The flight to the airport *Cortez* took about five hours and they arrived around noon. The rented car was there and they drove to the hotel, located in *Mesa Verde National Park* on a high shoulder of Mesa Verde, offering panoramic vistas in to three states. It was quiet enough to hear the ravens fly by. It was a place to linger and appreciate why people lived there of seven centuries. After having a hearty lunch at the hotel restaurant, they decided for that day to walk around and know the neighborhood. The park looked like without borders and many people seemed to enjoy just a pleasant walk in that afternoon, without searching for historical sites. Lara and Thad, holding hands, paced along the alleys, admiring the rich environment that seemed to be unique. Back at the hotel, they planned a rigorous schedule for the next day, starting with a visit to the *Chapin Mesa Archeological Museum*. Early in the morning, they went there and had a big cultural lesson about displays of dioramas illustrating

Ancestral Pueblo life. There were also many exhibits of prehistoric artifacts, and a chronology of Ancestral Pueblo culture. Next on their agenda was the *Cortez Cultural Center* containing a wealth of information on archaeology and Native American culture. The Center's Museum displayed interpretive exhibits on the Basketmaker and Pueblo periods of the Ancestral Pueblo people. Most interesting to visit was the *Sun Temple* which according to the modern Pueblo Indians it was a ceremonial structure, that was built using the same basic geometry found in ancient monuments from Greece to Egypt. For the next day, a guided tour to one of the most interesting sites anticipated the learning about so called "*Cliff Dwellings*" where during the late twelfth century many Ancestral Pueblo people began living in pueblos they built beneath the overhanging cliffs. Indeed, it was a site never before imagined that could exist.

In that long vacation for about one month, Lara and Thad had the most rewarding time, never expected to be so gratifying for both of them. Not only that they learned a lot about historical places and ancient cultures, but they shared tremendously strong feelings for each other and of being emotionally close together more than before. In the last day of their sojourn, they went to visit one of the gift shops, featuring regional Native American handcrafts where a big display showed beautiful, handcrafted jewelry featuring silver and turquoise available from many Southwestern tribes, especially from the *Navajo* tribes for whom the color turquoise represents happiness, luck, and health. Thad bought for Lara a finely wrought ring with silver and turquoise and put it on her finger as a symbol of his love.

"I'll take it off when my finger will be cut off."

He kissed her with all the love he ever had for someone in his life.

They returned home with a deeper feeling of assurance that they will never be able to live apart from each other.

All in all their lives seemed to become peacefully, without major problems, and their dependence on each other established the most harmonious bonds between them. One day, Thad asked the big question which persisted in his mind for a long time:

"Will you marry me?"

Lara stared at him with wide-open eyes.

"Is it something wrong with our living together arrangement?"

"Nothing is wrong with that but being married means a stronger bond between us which will never be broken."

"I can feel a sense of insecurity, and I resent this, because I thought the bond between us is strong enough to resist the trend of all future events, some of which might become an emotional or circumstantial upheaval in our lives."

"In my secluded world that I built over the years, I feel lonely and without wings. Many of my thoughts and feelings I cannot share with you, because they are deeply buried and I'm unable to bring them up. Yes, our arrangement of living together is socially acceptable, but many times I feel like a stranger. I need my world to meet yours and become a whole unity. Being married to you, makes me feel confident that we can reach together a harmonious whole that will never have the slightest fracture to hurt our lives."

"Oh, dear, what am I going to do with you? Let's then get married and make that whole unity you are longing for, in your marvelous way."

He jumped like a small child and kissed her with adoration like worshiping her.

"You are a brilliant surgeon, and I thought you are more realistic, but you just proved to me that your sensibility is more acute than I knew."

"Next week we'll get married and now let's put an end to the analysis of my emotional perceptions."

Lara called Adam and Ami, and told them about her new prospective. They both were thrilled.

The next weekend, Thad had to go the Institute to check on one of his patients when Lara received a call from the emergency ward of the nearby hospital. Thad had an accident and the doctor found her number in his wallet and called her urgently. She felt like losing her sanity, and rushed to the hospital. The doctor told her from the police report, that a big truck ran a red light and hit him on the driver's side. He was very badly injured, had a concussion, his right leg was broken, had a shoulder dislocation, two cracked ribs, and his entire body was covered with bruises.

Lara felt like the entire world collapsed around her.

"You can see him if you want, but he is in a coma", the doctor said.

Lara went inside the room, barely keeping up on her feet. Thad looked like dead with all his body bandaged and wrapped in tubes and wires.

"You know who he is?", she asked.

"Yes. He is the brilliant surgeon Thadeus Barlos from the Research Institute of Reconstructive Surgery. We called the Director of the Institute, told him about the accident, and he wants him to be transferred to their hospital. He will send two doctors who will check on him and they will decide if he can be moved. This is all about I can tell you now. You can go home and I'll give you a call and let you know about what will be next."

"I'll stay here and wait as long as it takes."

She called Adam, who in less than ten minutes was there.

"Don't say anything because I don't want you to tell me what you don't know and what I might expect. I only can tell you that I feel like being crashed."

After an hour, the two doctors from the Institute decided to transfer Thad to their hospital where he could have the best treatment and care, and where he knew everybody from the medical staff. Lara and Adam followed the ambulance and went inside. Thad was placed in the emergency ward and surrounded by doctors and nurses in a room with the most advanced technology where digital communication tools allowed nurses and clinicians to uncover and track data in real time and adjust the course of treatment. A team of three doctors worked on Thad's body more than four hours, trying to revive his consciousness without any progress.

One of the doctors came out and told Lara and Adam:

"I am Doctor Josh Mueller, the chief of the trauma team. I would like to keep you updated with the actual condition of Doctor Barlos. He has a concussion that in good time might go away and his mental faculties will be restored. He has a spleen rupture that we operated and will heal without complications. His fractured bones of shoulder and leg are put back in their position and we prevented any movement until they heal. Even if it's too early for a definitive diagnosis, I must prepare you for the worst scenario. His left leg might remain paralyzed from the waist down, and he might be in wheelchair for the rest of his life. Later, we'll try on him the most modern medical therapy and maybe in time we might succeed to improve his condition. As I said, now it's too early to make any assumption. We'll keep him here under the most promising treatment and care that will prove to be effective. If you have questions please feel free to ask me."

"Thank you Doctor Mueller for everything", Adam said. "It is a very hard time for our family and we need to talk over and understand this grave situation. One of us will be here almost every day, close to him, and make him sure when he wakes up, that nothing can keeps us apart."

"I'll be here anytime you need me."

Lara was unable to speak a word; she was devastated. Adam took her to his home, where Ami make her feel better and taking care that she had everything around to make her comfortable, especially making her feel that she had her family close and loving her.

"You both are very considerate, and show me your care and love, but I want to go home and be alone with my thoughts and my feelings. I have to sort out many of my emotions that are overwhelming and I need to find my courage to be strong in case I have to face the worst. I only can do all these if I am home with the feeling that he is around."

"We both want to share with you our happiness even if this is not the right time to tell you, but we thought that every good news will help you", Ami said. "I'm pregnant, Mom. Justin is already six months old and we thought that it will be good to have another baby and have them both grow up together from this early age."

"Oh, dear Ami, this is news that I can afford to take at any time no matter how bad I feel. I'm enormously happy for you both."

They all embraced each other and Lara went home.

She went to the study, opened her books, and started a new research paper to publish. Her mind was unable to concentrate on reading, and it took her a lot of time just to write a few lines. She still had one month of vacation ahead, but she knew that her entire mental activity would bring all her efforts only around Thad. The next morning she went to the hospital, hoping for the best, and thinking of the worst. Thad was in the same condition without showing any change for improvement. Doctor Mueller was there with other two medical specialists in sensory and motor paralysis. Their prognosis was still an educated guess, since it was too early for them to know how Thad will respond to treatment. They all waited for him to come out of the coma and analyze his state of mind before going any further. Lara came close to him, took his hand, and started talking like if he could hear her. She told him about the many good moments they had together, about how much they used to chuckle at jokes told by their friends or have a big laugh sometimes without any grounds, at people trying to be amusing. She talked about their beautiful vacation when they felt so close and showed their love to each other like never before. Hoping that he will open his eyes, she brought with her lots of pictures they both took on the beautiful sites they visited. She told him how much she wanted him to come home and be with her, holding her tightly in his arms. She talked to him until she felt exhausted, hoping to see a sign of life that would be at least a slight hope for her and for the doctors.

Every single day she did the same, for more than three weeks. One early morning, Doctor Mueller called her and said that he opened his eyes and tried to put some words together. Lara rushed to the hospital as if she was out of her mind for so much excitement that she couldn't control, and which brought her new rising hopes.

"You have only ten minutes to stay with him",

Doctor Mueller said. "I don't want him to get excited. Let's take one step at the time."

"I'll do everything you ask, Doctor Mueller."

"Call me Josh. I watched his marvelous procedure when he operated on you. He said that you are his *Galatea* and one day he will marry you. I have your picture in my office, Lara. May I call you Lara?"

"Yes, Josh, you can call me whatever you want."

"Let's go inside and see him."

They went into the room, and when Thad saw Lara he smiled and stretched one arm toward her. She kissed his forehead and took his hand, trying in the same time not to start crying.

"I missed you at home and I keep my eyes all the time on the door, expecting you to come in. The kids miss you all the same."

"Let me look at you. I haven't seen you in a long time. Just looking at you makes me feel better."

"I'll be here with you waiting for you to get better and take you home where you belong with me."

"We'll have to wait for a while, my dearest, the doctors here said that I have to enjoy their hospitality until they will decide what to do with me."

"Visit is over for today", the nurse said.

Lara kissed him and promised to come the next morning. Outside the room, Doctor Mueller told her:

"We are going to move him upstairs in a private room where he will be more comfortable. Be patient, Lara, it takes time for him to show improvement."

"I'll be here tomorrow, Josh."

Lara went home, trying to concentrate on her papers, when Adam came in. She told him everything, mentioning that she will never let her hopes in his full recovery, to fail her.

"Maybe we should call other specialists from outside to consult him and see what their opinion might be", Adam said.

"We can do this, but for now he has to show some improvements after being in a coma for three weeks. I'll talk to his doctor tomorrow."

The next day, Lara went upstairs where Thad was moved to a private room, all equipped with a complicated system of instruments, apparatuses and screens to monitor each of his movements. His body was enwrapped in tubes and wires, and a team of doctors followed on screens his responses to treatment. They let Lara to have a few minutes alone with him.

"Did you come to see how crippled I am?"

"I came to tell you how much I love you and how much I want you to come home."

"This is my home, and I'll never have another one. I'm a doctor as you know, and it's not hard for me to understand exactly what I have to expect. Go home, Lara, and don't come again."

"We'll be married as we planned and I'll never give up on you. Remember how much we both wanted to join our lonely worlds into one and walk together side by side forever?"

"There will be no marriage and no one world for us. You have yours, and I have mine, and they will never join. Go home where you belong, and don't come back here, where I belong."

He closed his eyes and didn't utter another word.

Outside, Doctor Mueller told her:

"It is natural for him to react the way he did. He knows exactly what to expect and he doesn't want to share with you his life as a crippled. We are going to try now a rehabilitative therapy, which is a combination of medication and physical stimulation to restore functions, improve mobility, relieve pain, and limit permanent physical disabilities on the pathways of his central nervous system. If he responds, he will be on his way to partial recovery. He will be able to make some steps helped with crutches but most of the time he will use the wheelchair. This is all I can promise to you. Don't give up on him, Lara. He needs you more than any therapy."

"I never will, Josh."

Lara had one more week until fall when the school year begins. Every single morning she was at the hospital but Thad gave strict orders not to let her in.

After her summer vacation was over, she continued to go to the hospital every evening and stay in the visitors' waiting room for one hour. Sometimes one of the doctors came and talked to her, other times she was alone, waiting in vain for one of the medical staff to come and say a word to her. Thad's condition was the same and the rehabilitative therapy seemed to have very little effect. One evening, Lara stepped over any orders, and went to his room.

"Get out, and go home. I told you never to come here. I don't need you, I don't love you, and I never loved you. If you got the wrong impression, now is the time to change it and be convinced that I never loved you and I never will."

"Shut up, Thad. I know this scene, and if you insist to play it, at least shout at me, like they do in the movies. You love me, I love you, and nothing will change, no matter what your condition will be. If you like to step on my nerves by rejecting me, you just do what you want. I'll be here, there, or wherever, always next to you, waiting for you to come home. You have plenty of time to put in order your thinking process. Goodbye, now."

She left with a strange feeling that this time he paid more attention to what she said. For the next two days, Lara didn't go to the hospital. She had to recuperate her strength and decide what to do next. Adam came late evening to see her and make sure that she was all right.

"I thought that we should call for help a specialist in spinal cord injuries, and maybe there is a kind of treatment that might improve his condition", she said.

"We'll do that, Mom. I'll go with you tomorrow, and we'll talk to Doctor Mueller. If there is any hope, he will tell us."

Next day, both went directly to the doctor's office and told him about their request.

"A procedure called 'Epidural stimulation' can be tried on him, but this is in a very early stage of experimentation. It is an application of a continuous electrical current to the lower part of the spinal cord.

The stimulation is carried out via a little chip which is surgically implanted over the protective coating of the spinal cord. The electrical current is applied at varying frequencies and intensities to specific locations on the lumbosacral spinal cord, corresponding to the dense neural bundles that largely control the movement of the hips, knees, ankles, and toes. With the participants, once the signal was triggered, the spinal cord reengaged its neural network to control and direct muscle movements. We do not do this procedure in our Institute, but we know where to ask for specialists who might come here and perform the operation. It is only up to Thad to decide if he is ready to take the risk of a procedure, which is in a very early stage of study and experimentation. He knows very well about this procedure but he didn't mention his intention to try it. If the operation is successful, the aftermath benefit could be a few minutes, or a week, or few months, or forever. All depends on the overall health of the patient and of the way his organism will respond."

"Let me talk to him", Adam said. "It is time for him to listen to somebody."

Adam went to see Thad and talked to him more than one hour. Nobody knew what they talked about, nobody asked, and nobody was curious to find out how Adam convinced him to try the only medical chance to make him stand on his feet, he still had.

In the coming week, a team of three doctors from the Spinal Cord Injuries Research Institute came over and checked Thad on every single spot of his body.

They decided to perform the operation in the coming week, after he will be thoroughly prepared for it.

In that day when the surgery was scheduled, Lara and Adam came together and waited in the visitors' room for more than two hours. A doctor came out and said:

"I'm Doctor David Williams. The operation went very well as I expected. Thad is heavily sedated now and in good care of Doctor Mueller and his medical staff. The initial period of recovery will take about two to three weeks with exercising and physical therapy, and this could be a painful period for him. It will take about six to eight weeks for a complete recovery until the ability of the spinal network will learn and improve nerve functions. The best I could do is to make him in short time to move his leg, standing up and walking. In spite of the highest expectations you might have, his left leg will be paralyzed from the waist down without any chance for being restored to its normal functions. He will have to carry a cane not so much for support, but to give him assurance against an eventual fall. If everything will go according to my presumptions, he will be able to practice surgery without any impediment. Thad is my good friend, we went together to medical school, and I care very much for him. If you have any questions please ask."

"Thank you for everything, Doctor Williams", Adam said, "we would like to know when he will be ready to come home."

"Not until complete recovery and not until he will

be confident about his movements. Being here, he will be under constant care and observation until I'll be completely satisfied with his progress. You have to wait for a little while."

"May we come and visit him?", Lara asked.

"This is up to him and up to Doctor Mueller. I don't have any objection."

"We both thank you very much for everything you did for him and for us", Adam concluded the conversation.

Lara kept coming every afternoon without seeing him. After about three weeks, Doctor Mueller told her that he showed a small improvement with help from therapy and started moving a little his leg. Every day Lara watched him from a small window making sure that he couldn't see her. After six weeks, he was able to move his leg without any support and could make a few steps showing a big improvement. One day, Lara entered the room and decided to have a long talk with him.

"I came to tell you that I never gave up on you, no matter how you feel about me. I'm waiting until your complete recovery and then I'll take you home."

"I told you never to come here again. Here is my home and I don't have another one. You must understand finally, that I am crippled and there is no recovery. The chip they inserted in me, could work for a very short time and then I'll be back in wheelchair. This is what you want?"

"I love you no matter how you look or how you walk. Remember what you said not long ago? '*I need my world to meet yours and become a whole unity. Being married to you, makes me feel confident that we can reach together a harmonious whole that will never have the slightest fracture to hurt our lives.'* Those were your own words and you made me believe them and trust you. I want to have what I deserve, and what you promise to give me."

"Yes, I remember and I wish I could keep my words, but I cannot. We'll never have a life together. My world is here and I have no right to seek for the unity with your world that I wanted so much to achieve. I don't want you to spend your life wasting time and strength, for keeping alive a crippled body who has no other wish than to be dead. Please try to understand and accept my determination to continue living here for as long as it will be."

"Well, then I concede your wish. You decided to make your own destiny, and I will not interfere ever again."

She turned around and left, without any other word.

Time went by and Christmas was there, without any perspective of new hopes for Lara. Adam and Ami prepared a big holiday celebration for the entire family to come over and have a joyous time together.

"I'm not coming. I feel like a need to be alone without any company."

"Why?", Adam asked.

"I'm tired and my frame of mind is not receptive to any jubilation. I'll stay home, listening to music, watching a movie, or reading a good piece of a literary work."

"You're not a good liar, Mom. You want to stay home, hoping for him to come. Thad is a big disappointment for me and even a bigger jerk."

"No, Adam, he is not. I would behave the same if I were in his place. His body is on its way to recovery but his soul is bleeding. He needs time to think and to sort out his deeply troubled feelings. He knows well that we need each other more than ever before, and he knows well that I really don't care how he looks or how he walks, because I love him. Maybe, he will come to his senses and one day, he will come home to me, where he belongs."

"I hope you're right, Mom. Now, please come and join us to celebrate Christmas. The entire family will be there and Beatrice, Ami's grandmother will come too. We need all of us to be together."

"Who is cooking? I know that is not Ami."

"She doesn't know how to cook. We have catered for everything and we'll have a fabulous feast."

The entire family was already there, showing a big joy for being all together after a long time. Suzie eloped and nobody knew where she was, while *Madame* went to Florida with Doctor Muirs for the holidays; there was no maid at home after she fired the last one. Beatrice and Lara showed by turns their big love to baby Justin who smiled and prattled all the time as if he knew how to cherish everyone's attention. The dinner was indeed a fabulous feast but Lara barely touched the food, while all the others looked as if they didn't have enough. Late evening they were ready to go home promising to each others to meet again soon.

Time went by, it was already middle of February, when Lara decided to pay a visit to Doctor Mueller.

"Thad achieved full recovery and last week he performed the first operation on a patient. He can walk, and move his joints, has no longer any pain, and seems to have learned how to avoid any discomfort. Doctor Williams came several times to check on his condition and his prognosis was that the implanted epidural stimulation device proved to be a big success and Thad has the best chance not ever to reject it. He can go home, and have with you the good life he deserves."

In that evening, Lara felt free from the anxiety she had for a long time. Thad had his life back and that was all she wanted for him, even if she was no longer part of it. She loved him dearly and she always will, but it seemed to her that he will never come back and she will never see him again. He left her with only moments of dear memories of them being together, which she will always remember and treasure. Their love was maybe unique in a marvelous world of their own, but seemingly not strong enough to overcome the hardships that turned out to be much too extensive.

In June that year, Ami gave birth to a beautiful baby girl who looked like a marvel to all. They named her *Sarah Beatrice* and she became the love of everybody including Justin who was already fifteen months old. In the same month, Adam took his "Doctor of Juridical

Science (J.S.D)" degree at only twenty-six years of age with the perspective to become the youngest Professor of International Law. Their lives went smooth, with bright and promising future for every one, and without any more difficulties to overcome.

One late evening, Lara came home from the library, and saw the entire house with the lights on. She started trembling and almost stopped breathing when she stepped inside. Thad was there, standing up on his both feet, and smiling.

"I worship you."

She ran into his stretched arms and almost fainted. With a barely audible voice, she managed to whisper:

"Hold me tightly and shout loud and clear to me that you are real and I'm not dreaming."

He held her tightly against his chest and with a soft voice, he said:

"My life without you is only a prolonged death. It took me a lot of time to learn that I don't need anymore my secluded world to join yours and make of both a whole unit. My life is here in a real world where you and I can go together hand in hand, loving each other, trusting each other, and building our future on a path of happiness that we both deserve. It took me a long time to realize that I resented everything I loved and cherished, only because I was unable to overcome the bitterness that made my soul bleeding. It took me a long time to believe that you loved me the way I was, and you never expected a miracle to make me better than I could be. I only want to share with you everything good or bad that will come to us, to let me love you, cherish you, and be with you in our real world of today, and for as long as it will be."

They got married in a small ceremony attended only by their close family.

"*Tomorrow* I have to perform an operation on a broken jaw."

"*Tomorrow* I have a very hard case to defend a big corporation."

"*Tomorrow* I have to uphold a woman in a divorce settlement."

"*Today I have my whole real world for as long as it will be.*"